# MOVE OR DIE!

"All right, folks, I know it's hard for you, but we have to get a wiggle on. If you rehitch some of the teams, there should be at least one ox for every wagon."

Nobody moved, not wanting to leave the grave. Most stood still as stone lions, staring at the new mound of dirt. Fargo hated to get rough with them, but there was no other way to save them.

"Damn it, people, stir your stumps!" he snapped. "What's done is done. Do you want the children to die, too?"

That finally goaded them into action. Feeling like a brutal mine foreman, Fargo began helping the women with their teams. But he vowed to move heaven and earth—if that was what it took—to punish every murdering son of a bitch who had attacked these helpless innocents.

# THE

# TRAILSMAN

## #344

# SIX-GUN
# GALLOWS

### by

## Jon Sharpe

A SIGNET BOOK

SIGNET
Published by New American Library, a division of
Penguin Group (USA) Inc., 375 Hudson Street,
New York, New York 10014, USA
Penguin Group (Canada), 90 Eglinton Avenue East, Suite 700, Toronto,
Ontario M4P 2Y3, Canada (a division of Pearson Penguin Canada Inc.)
Penguin Books Ltd., 80 Strand, London WC2R 0RL, England
Penguin Ireland, 25 St. Stephen's Green, Dublin 2,
Ireland (a division of Penguin Books Ltd.)
Penguin Group (Australia), 250 Camberwell Road, Camberwell, Victoria 3124,
Australia (a division of Pearson Australia Group Pty. Ltd.)
Penguin Books India Pvt. Ltd., 11 Community Centre, Panchsheel Park,
New Delhi - 110 017, India
Penguin Group (NZ), 67 Apollo Drive, Rosedale, North Shore 0632,
New Zealand (a division of Pearson New Zealand Ltd.)
Penguin Books (South Africa) (Pty.) Ltd., 24 Sturdee Avenue,
Rosebank, Johannesburg 2196, South Africa

Penguin Books Ltd., Registered Offices:
80 Strand, London WC2R 0RL, England

First published by Signet, an imprint of New American Library,
a division of Penguin Group (USA) Inc.

First Printing, June 2010
10 9 8 7 6 5 4 3 2 1

The first chapter of this book previously appeared in *Texas Hellions,* the three hundred
forty-third volume in this series.

Copyright © Penguin Group (USA) Inc., 2010
All rights reserved

 REGISTERED TRADEMARK—MARCA REGISTRADA

Printed in the United States of America

# The Trailsman

Beginnings . . . they bend the tree and they mark the man. Skye Fargo was born when he was eighteen. Terror was his midwife, vengeance his first cry. Killing spawned Skye Fargo, ruthless, cold-blooded murder. Out of the acrid smoke of gunpowder still hanging in the air, he rose, cried out a promise never forgotten.

The Trailsman they began to call him all across the West: searcher, scout, hunter, the man who could see where others only looked, his skills for hire but not his soul, the man who lived each day to the fullest, yet trailed each tomorrow. Skye Fargo, the Trailsman, the seeker who could take the wildness of a land and the wanting of a woman and make them his own.

*Southwest Kansas Territory, 1860—*
*where "Bleeding Kansas" earns its name in spades*
*when Skye Fargo cleans out an outlaw hellhole.*

# 1

The Ovaro suddenly gave his trouble whicker, and Skye Fargo, naked as a newborn, shook water from his eyes as he hustled out of the chuckling creek and onto the grassy bank.

His gun belt hung from the limb of a scrub oak, and he filled his hand with blue steel. He clapped his hat on, not wanting to die totally naked. Then he knocked the rawhide riding thong off the hammer and thumb-cocked his single-action Colt.

"Steady, old warhorse," he soothed the nervous pinto stallion. "Let's have a squint—might be just a stray buffalo spooking you."

Staying behind the stunted tree, Fargo used his left hand to clear his vision of leaves. His face was tanned hickory nut brown above the darker brown of his close-cropped beard. Eyes the bottomless blue of a mountain lake peered out from the shadow of his broad white plainsman's hat.

Fargo's first glimpse was the infinite vista of the western Kansas Territory plains, so vast and boundless that many men lost their confidence for feeling so dwarfed in it.

A heartbeat later, however, his blood iced when he saw that trouble was boiling to a head.

About a quarter mile north of his well-hidden position at the creek, a small group of pilgrims—perhaps seven families—were traveling west. Fargo recognized their sturdy wagons as the type made famous in Lancaster County, Pennsylvania. And the men's clergy-black suits, the women's crisp white starched bonnets, told him they were Quakers.

Pacifists, out here of all places. Fargo mocked no man for his heartfelt religious convictions and tended to like the hardworking, charitable Quakers. But this was the wrong place to turn the other cheek.

*1*

And most definitely the wrong time, he thought, watching a boiling yellow-brown dust cloud approaching from the Cimarron River to the north—a large group of riders, and only iron-shod horses would kick up that much dust. Large groups of riders, anywhere in the Kansas Territory, meant hell would be coming with them. This wasn't called Bleeding Kansas for nothing.

"You damn, thick-skulled fools," Fargo said in frustration as he pulled on his buckskin shirt and trousers, then his triple-soled moccasin boots. "This ain't Fiddler's Green out here."

Fargo knew there had been settlement going on for some time in the eastern half of the territory, but lately he had seen more pilgrims like these pushing way too far west—well beyond the U.S. Army's protection line. Just some stubborn and isolated homesteaders trying to prove up government land, without permission, in rain-scarce country better suited for grazing.

The Quakers, having spotted the approaching riders, had reined in their teams of oxen. But since defending themselves was not an option, they took no further action—merely waited patiently for whatever fate befell them.

By now Fargo's stomach had fisted into a knot. The riders were close enough that he recognized their butternut-dyed homespun clothing. Border ruffians . . . organized gangs of supposed anti-slavers who clashed with the "pukes," similar gangs from Missouri who used pro-slavery rhetoric as a thin excuse to terrorize settlers.

Fargo had waltzed with both factions before: kill-crazy marauders of no-church conscience.

But usually, he reminded himself, they were found well east of here, where the settlers and towns were. This was a long distance from their usual range—a fact that piqued Fargo's curiosity.

"Something ain't jake here, old campaigner," he told the Ovaro, his voice calming the nervous stallion.

First Fargo heard the warbling cries as the attackers moved in, then the sickening sound of a hammering racket of gunfire. Men frantically pushed their women and children into the wagon beds as bullets dropped some of the oxen in their traces.

At least thirty riders, Fargo estimated, all well-heeled and liquored up. And he knew damn well these mange pots could take a human life as casually as shooing off a fly. Many had devel-

2

oped a taste for killing during that slaughterfest known as the Mexican War.

After killing a number of the oxen, they took aim at the butcher beef and milk cows tied to the tailgates of the wagons. Fargo's face etched itself in stone when they next killed every adult male, then pulled some of the screaming girls from the wagons and gang-raped them—innocent girls who had never experienced violence in their lives.

But Fargo stayed hidden despite the anger roiling his guts. It was one of the ugliest scenes he had ever witnessed, but there wasn't a damn thing he could do about it—not now.

He had learned long ago never to push if a thing wouldn't move. He would gladly risk his life to help any man—and especially a woman or child—if there was even the slimmest chance of success. Revealing himself now, however, would simply make him part of the slaughter. Fargo preferred to survive so he could avenge it.

And he vowed that he would. He had been on his way to the sand-hill country of the northern Nebraska Panhandle country, hired by the U.S. Army to be a fast-messenger rider between military outposts there. But the army could wait—no man worth the name could turn his back on this.

The grisly nightmare was over in about fifteen minutes. At least the marauders hadn't killed any women or children. When the attackers had cleared out, after only quickly looting the wagons, Fargo untied the Ovaro's rawhide hobbles and vaulted into the saddle.

"Jesus, I could use a drink," he informed the landscape as he cleared the scrub oaks and cantered the Ovaro toward the scene of devastation.

The sights—and especially the god-awful sounds—forced Fargo to all his reserves of strength. The survivors had gathered around dead and dying men, their cries piteous. Girls who had been brutally raped lay in wide-eyed shock, young children bawled like bay steers, frightened out of their wits. Despite his best effort, Fargo misted up.

An elderly woman spotted him riding in and screamed. "Please, God, no more!" she begged the heavens. "Thou must please make him leave us alone!"

Fargo realized she had confused his fawn-colored buckskins with butternut.

"I'm a friend, ma'am," he assured her. "I'm not part of that bunch that just left."

"Friend?" she repeated in a tone implying she no longer trusted the word. Then she turned away and folded to the ground, overcome with grief.

A man lay slumped on the box of his wagon, screaming in agony. Fargo hauled back on the Ovaro's reins and threw a leg over the cantle, dismounting. He threw the reins forward to hold his pinto, and then checked on the man. He'd been gut-shot twice and was past all help. All that lay in store for him was hours of indescribable agony while he bled out.

His face set hard as a steel trap, Fargo moved out of the man's line of sight, shucked out his Colt, and sent the man to glory with a clean head shot. He expected howls of protest, but this bunch was in such shock no one took notice.

"Listen, folks!" Fargo shouted. "We'll have to bury your dead and get you out of here. Even if that gang of white men is done with you, the Indian Territory is only forty miles south of here, and some of the hotheads like to jump the rez. There's dozens of tribes there, and warpath braves could be anywhere in this area."

No one seemed to be listening. Fargo grabbed a shovel from a wagon and began digging a mass grave. Soon a few women and older boys had joined him. The elderly woman Fargo had first spoken to had recovered from the worst of her shock and spoke a prayer after the bodies had been covered with dirt.

"We thank thee, young man," she said to Fargo. "We came out from western Pennsylvania. We never expected anything like this. No one warned us. We're just farmers."

Fargo felt a welling of hopelessness. How many times had he heard those fateful words on the lips of green-antlered settlers burying their dead?

"What brought you folks this far out, ma'am?"

"Well, all the talk of railroads. We hoped to prosper."

Fargo had all he could do not to curse. There were still no railroads west of the Missouri River, but plenty of misguided folks were riding west on rumor waves. In 1854 the Committee on Territories proposed building three transcontinental lines, two of them slicing through the entire width of Kansas. Squatters immediately began pouring into the area. Some were the usual profiteers who hoped to cash in by being first on the scene. Others, like these folks, were hapless farmers expecting new markets for their crops—and finding only a nameless grave like this one.

But Fargo looked at this tired old woman, her eyes watergalled from weeping, and dropped the matter.

"Ma'am, obviously you folks are in no shape to push on. Fifteen miles east of the Cimarron River there's a trading post called Sublette. There's clean water, plenty of room to camp, and plenty of protection if you join with other settlers. There's also experienced guides for hire if you decide to go home."

The woman nodded. "My name is Esther Emmerick. Who were those men who . . . who attacked us?"

Again that question niggled at Fargo. "Well, they sure looked like Kansas border ruffians. But this is mighty far west for them."

"I've heard of them—supposedly they are looters. These men hardly touched our possessions."

"Yeah, I noticed that, too," Fargo said. "It's a mite curious, isn't it?"

The old matriarch steeled her resolve with a mighty sigh. "We're in God's hands for good or ill. Will thou take us to this trading post, Mr. . . . ."

"Fargo. You better believe I will. I'm on a mission for the U.S. Army, but it can wait."

"Army? Thou are a solider?"

"No, ma'am. I do contract work for them now and then. Scouting, hunting, messenger, in that line."

"I see. One moment, please, Mr. Fargo."

The woman went to a nearby wagon, rummaged in the back, and returned with a doeskin pouch. It was sewn shut with thick gut string.

"Two nights ago," she explained, "a badly wounded soldier, barely able to walk, met up with our group. The poor man died, but before he did he gave this to my—my husband—"

Her eyes cut to the new grave, but then she forged on. "He could barely speak, but he said it was imperative that this pouch be delivered to a military officer—any officer. He said it must not be opened before such delivery. Thou, Mr. Fargo, are more likely to see an officer before I do. May I trust it to thee?"

Fargo took it, noticing dried blood all over it. "It feels empty," he remarked.

"Yes, but that poor soldier was adamant that it be delivered."

"I'll take care of it," Fargo promised.

He glanced around. A westering sun threw long, flat shadows to the east.

"All right, folks, I know it's hard for you, but we have to get a wiggle on. If you rehitch some of the teams, there should be at least one ox for every wagon."

Nobody moved, not wanting to leave the grave. Most stood still as stone lions, staring at the new mound of dirt. Fargo hated to get rough with them, but there was no other way to save them.

"Damn it, people, stir your stumps!" he snapped. "What's done is done. Do you want the children to die, too?"

That finally goaded them into action. Feeling like a brutal mine foreman, Fargo began helping the women with their teams. But he vowed to move heaven and earth—if that was what it took—to punish every murdering son of a bitch who had attacked these helpless innocents.

# 2

Rafe Belloch, hidden in an erosion gully north of the attack site, studied everything through a pair of German-made field glasses.

"Christ on a crutch," he muttered softly. "That's all I needed."

"What's wrong, boss?" Shanghai Webb asked.

"Plenty," Belloch replied, still peering through the glasses. He was tall and whipcord thin, with a high pompadour, a thin line of mustache, and a pointed Vandyke beard.

Belloch took in the magnificent black-and-white pinto, the tall man's buckskin clothing, and the brass-framed Henry rifle protruding from the man's saddle scabbard.

"I could be wrong," he said, "but I think that jasper helping those Quakers is Skye Fargo."

"So what? Whoever that is, he's just one man." Shanghai was a barrel-chested, rawboned man with long, greasy black hair tied in a knot between his shoulder blades. Unlike his boss, whose only visible weapon was a thin Spanish boot dagger, he wore a brace of pistols and a bowie knife.

"No," Belloch corrected him. "If we're not careful, he's the rock we'll all split on. That son of a bitch is death to the devil. But we'll bide our time and soon Fargo will be worm fodder."

Two more men, Moss Harper and Jake Ketchum, had just joined Rafe and Shanghai in the gully. Both wore the cutaway holsters of professional gun-throwers.

"Hell, why wait at all?" demanded Moss. "Best way to cure a boil is to lance it. Me, Jake, and Shanghai can pop the bastard over right now."

Rafe's thin lips twitched into a smile. "All three of you boys have a set on you, all right. That's why I chose you over the rest as my field lieutenants. But even three good men won't take down Skye Fargo—not on the open plains."

7

Moss grunted. He had thinning red hair, a crooked nose broken in two places, and a patch over his left eye, which had been shot out in the Mexican War. "Happens he's so rough, how's come he didn't try to help them mealymouthed psalm singers when it would've mattered?"

"Men like him, who live their entire lives on the frontier, don't stay alive by tilting at windmills. But you can take *this* to the bank: He won't ride away like it's none of his business. It's an account he means to settle."

"All right," Shanghai said. "You want I should catch up with the rest of our men? He can't whip thirty at once."

"No, it's too risky."

"Boss, has your brain gone soft? We can catch him in fifteen minutes and shoot him to rag tatters."

Belloch lowered the glasses and looked at him. His hard, dark eyes pierced like a pair of bullets. "Evidently you lads don't recognize the name Fargo. You might know him better as the Trailsman—that's what some call him."

"The Trailsman," repeated Jake Ketchum, a wiry and small man with a mean little face like a terrier. A string of leathery human ears dangled from his rattlesnake-skin belt. "Yeah, I've heard some saloon gossip."

"In his case it's not gossip. He's got more guts than a smokehouse, and he rides the fastest, strongest horse in the West. Our men's horses are stale by now, they'd never catch him at a dead run. Even if they could get close, Fargo's a dead shot with that Henry rifle of his. That's—what?—sixteen accurate shots from a repeater. And they say he can knock the eyes out of a buzzard at two hundred yards."

Shanghai snorted. "Yeah, and oysters can walk upstairs, too. No offense, boss, but since when did you turn into a nervous Nellie who believes in Robin Hood? Sounds like this lanky bastard puts ice in your boots."

"No man does that, Shanghai. But there's a right way and a wrong way to go about killing a man like Skye Fargo. We're going to do it the right way—and before he turns that mystery pouch over to the U.S. Army."

"Pouch?" Shanghai repeated. "What's in it?"

"That's why I employed the adjective 'mystery.' Some old

8

Quaker crone gave it to him. They're all headed east now, probably to Sublette."

"Might be it's nothing to do with us," Moss suggested, adjusting his eye patch.

Rafe shrugged. "Yes, maybe it's just her family recipes, eh? But she gave it to Skye Fargo. And that tells me it's likely to be trouble—the worst kind in the world. The kind that leaves men dancing on air."

Shanghai paled under the dust coating his face. "You don't mean . . . the senator?"

Rafe nodded. "I have no idea, mind you, but that's what I suspect."

"Mr. Belloch," Jake put in, "speaking of that deal with the senator, there's something I don't quite savvy. You work for the Kansas Pacific, ain't that right?"

Belloch kept a poker face. "I draw pay from them, Jake, yes."

"Then how's come we're raising hell in these parts? Ain't this close to the route they favor?"

"Jake, you flap your gums too much," Shanghai cut in. "You got some problem with your pay?"

"Hell no."

"Good. Just shut your gob and carry out orders."

"Sorry for nosing in, Mr. Belloch," Jake said in a contrite voice. "You're the rainmaker in these parts."

Belloch flashed his thin-lipped smile. "Rain, sleet, snow, and sunshine. But, boys, never mind me," he said. "Don't you realize there's been a horrifying massacre here today?"

Shanghai's eyes narrowed. "You been grazing locoweed? *We* done the massacre."

"Shush." Belloch touched a finger to his lips. "Boys, it was shocking and we all saw it. Skye Fargo, dressed like a border ruffian, led a band of desperadoes against those poor defenseless Quakers and killed their menfolk. Even violated their girls. Then he had the brazen effrontery to slip off, change back into buckskins, and pretend to help them."

"What's brazen frunnery?" Jake asked.

"Gall, Jake, gall. The murdering bastard is widely known as a railroad hater. That must be why he did it. And we, being only four in number, were helpless to prevent it."

Shanghai grinned, revealing a few stumps of tobacco-stained teeth. "Boss, you are some pumpkins. That's pure genius."

"I'll write up a report for the dispatch rider, and we'll all sign it," Belloch added. "Under territorial law, and with my credentials, that'll be excuse enough to shoot him down like a rabid wolf."

"There's still that pouch," Moss pointed out.

Belloch nodded. "From now until we kill him, Skye Fargo is the man of the hour. Since he's known to work for the U.S. Army, I suspect he intends to deliver that pouch to a military man. Come hell or high water, we're going to prevent him."

Fargo knew he was being watched, but out on the Great Plains that never worried him much.

He never felt as relaxed, anywhere in the West, as he did on the open plains—still foolishly known as Zebulon Pike's Great American Desert in geography books back east. There were dangers, to be sure. In some places rattlesnakes bred unchecked, and he had seen horse and rider suddenly consumed by them as if in flames, a writhing mass that brought death in seconds.

And up from deep Texas there were wild herds of man-killing longhorns and equally lethal mustangs. The mustangs "liberated" saddle horses, stranding men to die in the vast lonesome. Fargo had encountered prairie-dog towns that stretched for miles, where grass knee-high to a tall man hid the holes so well a rider could lame his horse without warning.

But human enemies were at a serious disadvantage out here. Ambush was nearly impossible, except in the growth near water, and the only real danger was large groups of attackers—and with a good Henry rifle like his, even they could be discouraged.

Still, especially after the brutal massacre he'd witnessed yesterday, Fargo kept his sun-crimped eyes in constant motion while he formed balls of cornmeal and water and tossed them into the hot ashes of his campfire to bake. Several hours after sunset yesterday he had ridden into Sublette with the survivors of the massacre. After resting and graining the Ovaro, he had headed west twenty miles or so to the Cimarron River and made camp.

He had been followed all the way by several men who kept their distance but made no effort to hide. Exactly why, Fargo wasn't sure. Maybe it had something to do with that mysterious pouch, although he wasn't sure how anyone could know he had it. At any rate, Fargo's ride north to the Nebraska Panhandle would have to wait—after what he witnessed yesterday, there was a blood reckoning coming.

At the moment, however, he had "visitors" closer to hand. Clumsy ones, at that. Once again he heard rustling noises from wild plum bushes near the river.

"Tell me, boys," Fargo called out. "You gonna hide in them bushes all day, or do you plan to shoot me? The suspense is killing me."

"Mister, we got you covered!" shouted the voice of an obviously young man. "We're coming out! If you go for that pistol, we'll make a sieve outta you!"

Fargo, chewing a hot corn dodger, fought back a grin. "That's mighty gaudy patter. By the way, this Colt is a revolver, not a pistol. Are'n'cha s'posed to shout out, 'Toss down your gun!'?"

After an awkward pause: "Toss down your gun!"

"Atta boy. But if you don't mind, I'll lay it down gently. These walnut grips damage easy."

Fargo lay his Colt in the grass and continued eating. The bushes rustled some more as two boys, barely on the cusp of manhood, emerged and moved cautiously toward him. Both lads were tall, gangly towheads with fair skin burned raw by the late summer sun. Clearly they were brothers, the eldest stronger in the chest and sporting some blond fuzz on his cheeks and upper lip.

The oldest one wagged a big Smith & Wesson Volcanic pistol at Fargo. "This here is a holdup, mister. Hand over your money."

Fargo fished a horseshoe nail from his shirt pocket and used it as a toothpick, still watching the boys. Both were severely underfed and wore flour-sack clothing, their floppy hats stained and burned from doubling as pot holders.

"You deef, mister?" the young man demanded. "Break out your money or it's curtains!"

*"Curtains?"* Fargo laughed. "So you two owlhoots are about half rough, is that it?"

He snatched his Colt out of the grass and blew the Volcanic out of the older brother's hand. Before it could hit the ground, Fargo shot it again, sending it off in another arc.

"Katy Christ!" the kid exclaimed. "That's fancy shootin', mister! Are you a gunfighter?"

"No, I generally earn my wages the honest way." Fargo twirled the Colt back into its holster. "Name's Skye Fargo. Who are you boys?"

"I'm Dub McCallister," the oldest said. "This here's my brother Nate."

"Both of you look like you just crawled out of three-cornered britches. Does your mother know you're out?"

Dub scowled. "I'm nineteen and Nate's seventeen. We're old enough to fend for ourselves."

"Yeah, I see that," Fargo said sarcastically. "Let me give you two 'road agents' a tip. Even with the hammer back, a pistol that's loaded should look dark as the inside of a boot when you look down the barrel. Yours has light streaming through it. You two best find another line of work—you're poor shakes as holdup men."

"Dub, you shitheel!" Nate lashed out. "I *told* you to cram some grass down the barrel!"

"Shut your piehole, clodpole, before I—"

"Both of you knock it off," Fargo snapped. "By right of territorial law, I can shoot the pair of you for cause."

Both towheads stood there looking miserable and ashamed. Fargo saw beggar lice leaping from their clothing. In spite of their poorly attempted crime against him, Fargo felt pity stir within him. He remembered his own shaky start when he was thrust wide upon the world at eighteen. These weren't cold-blooded criminals—they were failed sodbusters on the brink of starvation.

"Sit down, boys, and get outside of some grub. You're no desperadoes; you're just hungry."

"Mr. Fargo!" they said in unison, hurrying to the fire and helping themselves. Fargo had intended to eat some of those corn dodgers cold in the saddle, but they were disappearing fast and he reminded himself he had plenty of jerked buffalo.

"Even if I had a bullet," Dub told him with a full mouth, "I wouldn'ta shot you, Mr. Fargo."

Fargo picked up the Volcanic and its broken cylinder promptly fell out.

"Yeah, I see what you mean," he scoffed. "This weapon ain't worth an old underwear button. What you've got here is a fistful of nothing. Do either of you know beans from buckshot?"

"Both of us can shoot," Nate said. "Our pa taught us 'fore he died. He fought Miami and Huron Indians back in Ohio."

"You got horses?"

"Yessir. Hid down by the river."

It was movement, not shape, that caught a man's attention in the open spaces. Fargo detected motion about a mile south, moving up the bank of the river. They weren't likely dry-gulchers—not on the open plains. He glanced at the saddle pocket where he'd stuffed that doeskin pouch. His suspicion was only a glimmer . . .

"Ohio?" he repeated. "Is that where you're from?"

"Yessir," Dub replied. "Hamilton County. Us, Pa, Ma, and our sister Krissy. Had us a farm there."

"I just can't put handles on this," Fargo said. "I've been to Ohio. It's good farmland. Rich soil and plenty of water. Why are farmers leaving it to come out here? It's not safe enough yet for families to roost here, and the rain is fickle."

"Pa could explain it to you if he was still alive," Dub replied. "Ma says he just had jackrabbits in his socks. Soon as you could see the nearest neighbor's light at night, Pa felt hemmed in and ready to push on."

Fargo grinned. "Now I can understand. But the Indian Territory is just south of us, and this area is crawling with white owl-hoots on the dodge. It's no place for tenderfoots who don't know sic 'em about the frontier."

Almost as if timed to prove Fargo's point, his hat suddenly spun off as a bullet whiffed in. A fractional section later, the solid crack of a big-bore rifle reached them.

Both boys leaped like butt-shot dogs, then pressed flat into the deep grass.

"Sharps rifle—known as the Big Fifty," Fargo said calmly, his face rueful as he studied this latest bullet hole in his hat. "The widow-maker, most dangerous gun on the Plains. And, right now, a damn good shooter using it."

"Ain't you gonna take cover?" Nate demanded, his voice tight with anxiety.

"Nah. It's a single-shot and he's reloading," Fargo said, ignoring his tack and leaping onto the Ovaro bareback. "They sent in their card, now it's time to send in mine."

Jacking a round into the Henry's chamber and grabbing a handful of mane, Fargo thumped the pinto with his heels and they shot off toward the Cimarron. The Trailsman held on with his muscular legs and aimed toward the spot where he'd last seen motion, peppering it with rounds. He expected return fire. Instead, two riders suddenly pulled foot from the trees before he even got close. Western rivers dried to trickle streams by September, and they easily forded the Cimarron, bearing west.

Fargo wasn't fool enough to close in too much on a Big Fifty in open country. He tugged on the Ovaro's mane and returned to camp.

"They ran like scared rabbits," Dub greeted him, flashing his gap-toothed grin. "How's come you run 'em 'steada hunkering down?"

"They expected me to cover down. Always try to surprise, mystify, and confuse your enemies."

"Yeah," Nate chimed in, "but they was shooting at you, and you headed right toward the gun."

"If you think about it," Fargo pointed out, "there's no sense in running a gun. You ever met a man who can run faster than a bullet? So come right out of the chute bucking—they don't expect it, and it rattles 'em. That's why they ran."

"Are you wanted by the law?" Nate added, sounding almost hopeful.

"Evidently I'm wanted, all right, but not by the law."

"Do you know who that was, Mr. Fargo?" Dub asked.

"Don't think so," Fargo replied as he swung down. "But lately this area is lousy with egg-sucking varmints. All I know is they've been watching me."

"I wonder how's come," Nate said.

"That's got me treed, son." Again Fargo glanced toward his saddle. "But it's possible they want something I have."

# 3

Fargo quickly ran a wiping patch down the Henry's bore, reloaded the tube magazine, then tacked the Ovaro for the trail.

"Where you boys headed?" he asked as he checked his cinches and latigos.

"Well, the thing of it is," Dub replied, "our farm is just ten miles west of here. But we can't go back."

"Why not?"

"On account it ain't a farm no more," Nate said, his voice bitter. "The wheat headed up real good, and the corn got its tassels. Then the goddamn grasshoppers ate us out."

"If we stay on," Dub explained, "won't be enough food for Ma and Krissy. So me and Nate are headed east to see can we maybe join the border gangs. Ain't much else we can do."

Fargo shook his head in disgust. "If youth but knew and age could do."

"What's that mean?" Nate demanded.

"Are you boys murderers? Are you the kind to rape innocent girls? Are you prepared to burn women and children and old men out of their homes in the middle of the night?"

"'Course not," Dub said, his tone resentful. "We cuss a mite, and chew, but we was Bible-raised."

Fargo described, in vivid detail, the raid yesterday by border ruffians on unarmed Quakers. He included the man he was forced to mercy kill. Both boys paled noticeably.

"Jumpin' Jupiter!" Nate said. "We heard they just robbed federal paymasters and such."

"Well, junior, you heard wrong. The border ruffians are the same trash that persecuted the Mormons and drove them out to Salt Lake. And what about your ma and sister? You two bravos just plan to leave two defenseless women out here alone among Indians and hard cases on the prod?"

"We was aiming to go back home," Dub said, "soon's we earned some money with the gangs."

"Besides," Nate chimed in, "they aren't defenseless. We left Ma the gun that works, and thanks to a favor Pa done for the Indians before he died, they leave our place alone."

After what he'd witnessed yesterday, Fargo doubted that anybody was safe out here—least of all the dying man he was forced to shoot. He looked at both of these boys—their ragged clothing, their emaciated frames, their desperate eyes—and realized what he had to do.

Fargo was flush with big winnings from an all-night poker game with officers at Fort Leavenworth, where he had just finished a stint as chief of scouts. It was far more than he required for his meager needs.

"So your place is pretty safe, huh?" he said. "Let's ride out and have a look at it."

Dub and Nate exchanged a wary glance. "You trying to trick us into going back, Mr. Fargo?" Dub asked.

"Look, boys, haven't I been a square dealer with you? You tried to rob me, and I gave you breakfast instead of lead in your sitters. Don't worry—even if I tricked you into going back, how could I make you stay?"

Dub slowly nodded. "All that's true. But—don't take offense, Mr. Fargo, but are you a gentleman? You see, our sister, Krissy, well, she's mighty easy on the eyes. And our ma still turns heads, too."

Fargo grinned. "You want me to ride in blindfolded?"

"Ahh." Dub flushed. "'Course you can look. Pa always told us you can't hang a man for his thoughts. But you won't . . . you know, outrage them?"

"If that means 'rape,'" Fargo said, "I ought to slap you sick and silly, you young dolt. If that was my plan, I'd just let you boys ride on and find the place myself. All my gals are willing volunteers."

"That's all we need to know."

With Fargo leading the Ovaro by his bridle, all three men headed on foot toward the river, Fargo carefully scanning the wide-open country around them. The McCallister boys had hobbled their mounts, two huge and gentle dobbins, or farm horses, in a willow copse near the river. Fargo noticed their saddles were just sheepskin pads, the bridles simple rope hackamores.

"Mr. Fargo," Nate said as the trio started across the nearly dry bed of the Cimarron, "why we going to our place?"

"Because I'm lucky at cards," Fargo replied cryptically, discreetly refraining from adding: *and with women*.

Rafe Belloch, whose fancy pebble-stock cards identified him as a "businessman's agent," had established his frontier headquarters ten miles east of the busy trading post at Sublette. It was a well-protected dugout in the middle of a thick pine copse, built decades earlier by French fur traders as a winter headquarters.

"I told both of you," he said in his quiet, menacing tone, "to just *watch* him for now. The point right now is simply to make sure Fargo doesn't get near any soldiers. Why, Moss, did you shoot at him?"

Moss Harper and Jake Ketchum stood in sullen silence just inside the dugout. A bottle of fine bourbon and a pony glass sat before Rafe on a crude deal table. Despite the rustic lodging, he wore a new wool suit and glossy ankle boots.

Moss tugged nervously at his eye patch. "I understood your order, Mr. Belloch. But I had a good bead on the son of a bitch, so I figured I'd just plant him in the bone orchard and get him out of your hair."

"Moss damn near plugged him, too," Jake added. "Blew his hat right off his head."

*You ignorant chawbacons*, Rafe thought. But he himself had recruited these men from the most ruthless of the border ruffians, and he knew they would cut out his heart if he berated them too severely.

"Well, it's too dead to skin now," he said dismissively. "Did he get a good look at either of you?"

"No, sir," Moss said. "He charged us, but we done like you said and skedaddled."

Rafe nodded. "A wise policy. Be patient with Fargo, gentlemen. When it comes to survival, he's what they call a huckleberry above a persimmon."

"Ah, I know his type," Jake said. "He reads his name in all them crapsheets and overrates himself." He stroked his cutaway holster. "I've sent nine men over the range with Patsy Plumb here, and Fargo will make it ten."

"Oh, we'll kill him," Rafe agreed. "But I suspect Fargo rarely sees a newspaper, so don't count on the overrating part. Send Shanghai in when you leave."

While Rafe waited, he stepped outside to glance around. Most of his "crew," as he called the border ruffians on his payroll, were hanging around the area, gambling and drinking. Many of these men had been recruited back east in the rough Baxter Springs area, a wild and woolly corner of the Kansas Territory, near the Missouri border, that settlers had learned to steer clear of.

Belloch knew this Baxter Springs bunch had no respect for authority, but they did respect whiskey and gold, both of which the railroad barons supplied generously. There were millions to be made by whoever got that transcontinental railroad contract, and the U.S. Congress would be exceedingly generous in granting land for the right-of-way—land the railroad could then sell at top dollar after luring ignorant settlers out west with lying slogans such as, "Rain follows the plow!"

Shanghai Webb's gravelly voice cut into his thoughts. "You want to see me, boss?"

"Let's go inside, Shanghai. I take it you've heard all about Moss Harper's botched attempt this morning to kill Fargo?"

Webb followed his employer into the cool dugout. "Yeah. Moss don't mean to be disrespectful, boss. He thought he had a plumb bead, is all, and he knew you were worried about that pouch."

Rafe waved a negligent hand. "Actually, I'm glad he took that shot. From what I know of Fargo, it'll keep him in this area. He's one for settling accounts. And we *want* him to stick around."

Shanghai nodded. "That rings right."

Rafe pushed the bottle of bourbon toward Shanghai, who took a long belt, then wiped his mouth on his sleeve. "Say, that ain't wagon-yard whiskey, is it? Anyhow, yesterday you started frettin' about how Fargo might take that pouch to a fort or outpost. Now you really think he'll stick around these parts? 'Pears to me he's a drifter, and he ain't got much stake in the game."

"You're spot on when you say he's a drifter. But after what he saw yesterday, I'm again of the opinion that he'll stick."

Shanghai said, "It's his funeral. So you mean he's a crusader?"

"Hardly, from what I hear and read. He'll ignore a certain amount of lawbreaking. Hell, he'll run afoul of the law himself. But the murder of unarmed Quakers . . . Like I said yesterday, he won't let it stand. Which means, of course, that he'll show up in Sublette."

"If he does, we'll powder-burn him. Our men control that place."

Belloch stroked his spade beard. "It might come to that. But openly killing Skye Fargo would quickly get noised about the entire West, and my employers wouldn't appreciate the notoriety. If we can lay hands on that pouch, Fargo has nothing on us."

"What about that little barn dance yesterday?"

"Oh, it's true he saw the massacre, but he didn't see either of us. Besides, I'm writing up a report right now for our dispatch rider. It will implicate Fargo in the massacre."

"I take your drift," Shanghai said. "But we don't even know what's in that pouch he's got."

Rafe paced the length of the dugout, hands clasped behind his back. "True enough. But think back to the . . . incident with Senator Drummond and General Hoffman on their congressional fact-finding mission."

"Think back? Hell, that's all you hear about in Sublette— how both of them have disappeared. A search party has gone out from the outpost at Two Buttes."

Belloch nodded. "That's part of the plan—the news *has* to get out about the supposed Indian threat this far south on the plains. But what I mean is, do you recall how many soldiers, besides the general, were guarding Senator Drummond?"

"Uh-huh, I counted 'em. Twelve."

"And after . . . the incident, how many bodies did we count?"

Shanghai hesitated, seeing the point. "Only thirteen total. So you're thinking that means . . . ?"

"Exactly. One may have slipped away. Now do you see why I'm 'fretting' about that pouch?"

Shanghai swallowed another jolt of bourbon. "Christ yes! If it's what you're thinking, we could be boosted branchward."

"Colorfully put. So we have to get that pouch. I want you to pick your best sneak thief and send him to see me. And one more thing—about Moss. You heard him ask me, yesterday, about working for the Kansas Pacific?"

"I wouldn't sweat that, boss. Moss is a deadly bastard when he's on the scrap, but he ain't got the brains God gave a piss-ant."

"Maybe not, but he's cunning in his way. If he ever figures out that you and I are actually helping the Rock Island Line win its northern route, and he tells the Kansas Pacific leadership, we'll never make it to trial."

Shanghai was about to reply when two border ruffians, dragging a young woman between them, appeared outside the dugout.

"Mr. Belloch?" said a man with a red beard stained by tobacco spit. "Got a reg'lar peach for you here. Feisty little bitch. Snatched her from—"

"Never mind where you got her," Belloch said, appreciatively eyeing the slender young blonde whose pretty face was a frozen mask of fear. "Nobody saw you?"

"Nary a soul."

Belloch took a chamois purse from his coat pocket and counted out five silver dollars for each man.

"You know where to put her," he said. "Who gave her that shiner?"

"I done it," redbeard said. "Couldn't be helped. After I done for her husband, she fought like a wildcat."

"I told you I don't like bruised fruit. Next time you grab one for me, punch her in the stomach. That takes the fight out of them."

"Yessir. Didn't think of that."

"No, you wouldn't have," Belloch said, his mild sarcasm wasted on the thug.

After the two men dragged her away, Shanghai cleared his throat.

"There's whores in Sublette," Rafe said, knowing where this was headed. "That's where the crew goes."

"I know, boss, but them bitches ain't even got any teeth left. This here gal is exter pretty."

"Rank has its privileges."

"Yeah, but . . . any idea when you'll be finished with her? I wouldn't mind—"

"I dally with them only one time, then wait for the next one," Rafe said impatiently. "And when I'm finished, I always make

**20**

sure they will never be able to report it—what the Indians call 'stoning them into silence.' You take my meaning?"

"Sure. Leave her for me, and soon's I'm done I'll put the quietus on her."

"Fine, but it will be a couple of days. I don't touch any woman who sports a bruise or cut."

"That one's worth waiting for," Shanghai said. "I'll keep the rest away from her."

"Business before pleasure. Right now put her out of your thoughts and concentrate on Fargo. I'm about to put the report out on the massacre he led yesterday, a report you, Moss, and Jake will sign with me. But that report won't be worth a rat's ass if that pouch he's carrying contains what I fear it does and we fail to seize it."

Rafe slid a watch from his fob pocket and thumbed back the cover. "Time's pressing. Go find your best sneak thief and send him to me."

# 4

The trio of riders topped a long, low rise, and Dub McCallister pointed straight ahead.

"That's our place, Mr. Fargo. Ain't much to brag about. You can see we didn't bother to harvest the fields."

"Drought stunted the crops," Nate put in, "and then grasshoppers done for us."

"Jesus, boys," Fargo said, gigging the Ovaro forward. "How can you live in that soddy? The roof's caved in."

"We don't," Dub said. "Ma hated it from the get-go. One day she was boiling up some cabbage and a rattlesnake dropped off the roof right into the pot."

"Moses on the mountain, she had a conniption fit," Nate recalled, laughing at the memory. "Krissy hated the soddy, too. Well, the first good harvest we had, Pa sold off the wheat to the army and had some planks shipped out. Built that barn you see," he added proudly. "The only by-God wooden barn in the west Kansas Territory, I'll bet. When Pa died, Ma said the barn was our new house."

"Just one end of it," Dub added. "The rest is still a barn."

As they drew closer, Fargo saw a woman in a blue broadcloth skirt and white shirtwaist—clean but faded to gray—step out of the barn holding a long Jennings rifle. However, when she took her eyes off Fargo and recognized her sons, she propped the weapon against the barn.

"Hey, Ma!" Dub called as they rode into the hard dirt yard. "We brought company. This here's Mr. Skye Fargo. Mr. Fargo, this is our ma, Mrs. Lorena McCallister."

"Skye Fargo," she repeated. "Skye is a nice front name. Matches those blue eyes of yours."

Fargo tipped his hat. "Thank you, Mrs. McCallister. Lorena is a mighty nice name, too."

As Fargo swung down, landing light as a cat, he got a better look at this farm widow. She put him in mind of many women he had seen on the plains. Still pretty, still shapely, but with weather-creased eyes that had seen too much. She was just starting to wilt, like a beautiful bouquet one day after the ball.

"Well, you two," she said, looking at her sons, "I thought you were going out to conquer the world? I figured maybe you were in China by now."

They slid off their tall horses, too embarrassed to meet her eyes. "Ahh, we . . . met up with Mr. Fargo," Dub explained, too ashamed to mention the botched robbery. "He wanted to see our place."

Her eyes narrowed in suspicion as she glanced at Fargo. "See our place—or see Krissy?"

"Anything that's here," Fargo said honestly. "Including the handsome woman I'm speaking with right now."

Lorena smiled. "I like men who're frank—they don't harbor secret motives. Well, if it's the place you wanted to see, you must be disappointed, Mr. Fargo. Wilfred, my late husband, used to say there's room to swing a cat in out here. I like the open spaces, but with their pa dead and buried, the children miss Ohio."

Something at one corner of the barn caught Fargo's attention. He walked closer to examine it. A Southern Cheyenne red-streamered lance had been stuck deep into the dirt. Its shaft was wrapped in a strip of vermilion-dyed rawhide.

"Who put that peace pole on your property?" Fargo asked.

"Chief Gray Thunder's band from south of the Republican River. My husband saved his son's life when he almost drowned in the Cimarron."

"Ever since, we ain't never been attacked by Cheyenne or Sioux," Dub put in proudly.

Fargo nodded. "That pole was a stroke of good fortune. But there's free-ranging Osage and Pawnee out here, too, and a bunch of tribes in the Indian Territory south of here that like to jump the rez."

"We see them sometimes," Lorena said. "But, so far, when they see that spear, they've left us alone. It's these white marauders I fear—gangs moving in from the Missouri border region."

"Speaking of white marauders, Ma," Nate said, "we had us a set-to with some earlier today. Mr. Fargo here run 'em off like scairt rabbits. You oughter see him shoot—he's a dead aim."

Lorena's eyes took Fargo's full measure. "I'm not surprised to hear that. He looks fit for duty, all right."

"It wasn't much of a scrape," Fargo gainsaid. For Lorena's sake he didn't add: *but I expect it will get worse for all of us.*

A musically feminine voice interrupted them. "Ma, you didn't tell me we had company."

Fargo watched a young woman around twenty years old come around the corner of the barn, a reed basket of wildflowers depending from one arm. She was one of the comeliest farmer's daughters Fargo had ever seen: tiny-waisted and ample-breasted, with pale skin like flawless lotion, big sea green eyes and a profusion of hair black and shiny as a crow's wing.

"Krissy," Lorena teased, "you started brushing your hair the moment you spotted Mr. Fargo. And I don't blame you. He's what they call a well-knit man."

*And you two*, Fargo thought, glancing back and forth between both attractive women, *are what they call an embarrassment of riches.*

"Ma!" Krissy protested, fluttering her lashes at Fargo. "Such talk is shameless!"

An old hound dog had followed Krissy around the corner.

"That's Dan'l Boone," Nate told Fargo. "He's old and lazy, but nobody sneaks up on us. He didn't bark at you because me and Dub was with you."

"I'm glad you have a good watchdog," Fargo said. "And I'm glad you two ladies have a peace pole in plain sight. But those white marauders you just mentioned, Mrs. McCallister—you're wise to fear them. I recommend you consider going back to Ohio, or at least east of the Mississippi River."

"I already know it was a mistake to try and farm here, Mr. Fargo. Drought and grasshoppers have taught me that."

Krissy waited until her mother wasn't looking, then gave Fargo a come-hither smile he could feel in his hip pocket. It took him a moment to regain his train of thought.

"No, all due respect—your mistake, Mrs. McCallister, was in

leaving the Land of Steady Habits. You're just too far west, or too soon, anyhow. There's no dependable law out here in the Territories. Soldiers are scarce as hen's teeth—scattered so thin they can barely protect themselves, and these stupid three-month enlistments mean they never learn how to soldier."

"Yes, I told my husband it was lawless out here, but he said there was law back east. So much that we were headed to the county poorhouse. They brought in tax assessors and started taxing us on horses, mules, cattle, even how many bushels of corn we harvested. Wilfred said the sun travels west and so would we."

Fargo grinned. "My stick floats the same way his did. And nobody has the right to order you around. But it's becoming a tinderbox out here, and it's best to either stay east of the Mississippi or go all the way to Oregon where there's safety in numbers."

Lorena shook her head stubbornly. "You mean well, Mr. Fargo, and you're probably right. But my man killed himself to scratch out this farm—worked so hard he died from a double hernia that putrefied his insides. My kids are big enough to do as they please, but I just ain't leaving."

"And I won't leave Ma," Krissy said, hungry eyes raking over Fargo. "Like the boys done."

"We didn't leave her, you dang liar," Dub snapped at his sister. "We set out to, well, earn some money for the family."

"Shush it, both of you," Lorena said, looking at Fargo again. "They're fine boys, Mr. Fargo. A bit thickheaded, but brave, honest, and faithful. Fine marksmen, too, thanks to my husband. Trouble is, Wilfred passed away before he really had a chance to finish turning them into frontiersmen. Come inside the barn a moment, there's something else I'd like to show you."

Fargo followed her inside, the light dim after the glaring afternoon sunshine outside. The far end of the barn was obviously living quarters, complete with an iron cook stove, several chairs and a table, and beds. Halfway inside, Lorena knelt and dug her hands into the straw. She raised a trapdoor. Fargo noticed that pitch had been applied to it to keep the straw permanently in place.

"Wilfred dug it originally as an Indian tunnel," she explained. "It runs straight behind the barn and comes out in a dry creek bed. You head about fifty feet to the left and there's a thick tangle of hawthorn bushes. They hide a small cave that Wilfred dug. So between Dan'l Boone, the peace pole, my Jennings rifle and this tunnel, we aren't exactly helpless females."

"Well," Fargo said, "it's ingenious, for a fact. I guess you ladies have survived this long without a man, you don't need one now."

"Oh, I wouldn't put it exactly that way," Krissy said.

Lorena chuckled. "You'll have to forgive the girl, Mr. Fargo. It ain't often we see a man as handsome as you. Or any other kind, for that matter."

"I take that as a compliment from both of you, ma'am," Fargo said, wishing like hell both these boys would turn into birds and fly away. It had been too damn long since he'd enjoyed the mazy waltz, and a tumble with either of these women was just the carnal tonic he needed.

"Anyway," Fargo added, pulling a rawhide pouch from his pocket, "sometime back I got into a poker game with some soldiers and skinned 'em good. I consider poker winnings found money, and I got no use for it. I'd be honored if you folks would accept it."

When Lorena refused to extend a hand, Fargo grabbed her wrist and extended it for her. He poured $100—five double-eagle gold pieces—into her palm.

"Mr. Fargo, we can't—"

"Like hell you can't. It's poker profits, not hard-earned pay. There's something else I been thinking about: these towhead boys of yours. You women could still use some protection, and they need to learn how to take care of themselves. It won't take long to mold good clay into good plainsmen. Why don't I start by taking both of them with me to the trading post in Sublette? We'll stock you up on dry and can goods and such."

"Say! you're whistling!" Dub exclaimed. "Me and you, Nate, real plainsmen!"

Lorena looked as if she'd woken up in the middle of a dream. "Mr. Fargo, I don't know how to thank—"

"Found money, Mrs. McCallister, found money, remember? The wages of sin. 'Nuff said."

"Well, don't you have to be somewhere?"

"The Nebraska Panhandle, but there's time," he replied, leaving it there.

But Fargo strongly suspected he would sign his own death warrant if he headed toward any military installation while that pouch was in his possession. Nor did he plan to leave this area until he put "paid" to an account—that remorseless slaughter he witnessed yesterday, a sight seared into his memory for life.

Fargo and the McCallister brothers rode east for about an hour, closing in on the Cimarron River. Fargo kept his eyes to all sides, looking for motion, not shapes.

"When you're in wide-open country," he told his companions, "don't focus your eyes too much on one spot. Let them take in everything—I call it letting the terrain come up to your eyeballs. And now and then, do this."

Fargo tugged rein until he was facing north. "I'm looking at everything ahead of us from my side vision. Sometimes that shows things front vision will miss. Good trick for flatlanders to remember."

"You expect more trouble, Mr. Fargo?" Dub asked.

"I always expect trouble, lad. That way you'll be ready for it. But now that you've brought it up—it's only fair to warn you that lead tends to fly around me."

"Hell, we seen that already," Nate said. "That's why we want to side you."

"Look, slip a noose on this 'side' business, why'n'cha? I'm a one-man outfit, and we ain't gettin' chummy. I told your ma I'd show you some trail craft, and I will try not to get you killed. Speaking of that . . ."

Fargo hauled back on the reins, lit down, and rummaged in his offside saddle pocket. He removed two handguns, giving one to each of the brothers.

"Dub, the weapon you're holding is a Colt Navy, single-action. You've prob'ly shot squirrel guns, but do you know what single-action means?"

"Yessir. After you shoot it, you have to cock the hammer back to rotate the next bullet into the chamber."

"Well, your pa taught you something, anyhow. Nate, your gun is a Lafaucheux six-shot pinfire revolver. It's French. Ever heard of pinfires?"

"No, sir."

"Instead of a hammer that strikes a percussion cap," Fargo

explained, "it shoves a long pin straight into a paper cartridge. Not a bad gun, but the cartridges are hard to locate."

"Lookit there," Dub said. "It's got a foldaway knife blade under the barrel."

"Good for nothing but cleaning fish," Fargo scoffed. "There's one serious drawback, Nate—paper cartridges go off too easy if you bang the weapon. So no cartridge under the hammer until you're ready to shoot."

"Where'd you get these guns?" Nate asked.

"Let's just say," Fargo replied, "that their former owners have no use for them now. Let's see how you boys do. Now, I don't expect a hit, just do your best. Dub, you first."

Fargo was convinced that these green-antlered farm boys couldn't likely hit a tent from the inside, so he pulled out his tin plate and flipped it high into the air.

Dub fired once, sent the plate spinning, thumb-cocked the Colt Navy in a heartbeat, fired again and made it hop even higher.

Fargo's jaw was still falling open in astonishment when Nate took over, likewise drilling the plate twice with two shots before it hit the ground.

"Holy Christ," Fargo said. "When your ma said you were good shots, she wasn't stretching the blanket, was she? Boys, excuse me while I pull my foot out of my mouth."

"Whatever trouble you're in, Mr. Fargo," Dub pressed eagerly, "can we side you now?"

Fargo picked up his plate, staring ruefully at the four bullet holes in it. "Well, gents, you may be green, but you're solid wood. It's getting too late to be riding into Sublette. We'll make a cold camp, and I'll sleep on it.You sleep on it, too. Like I said—lead tends to fly around me."

# 5

Fargo picked a tree-sheltered area beside the Cimarron River for their camp that night. The three riders rubbed down their horses and put them on long tethers so they could graze during the night.

"If we had a fire going," Fargo explained, "that would mark our location for an enemy. So we'll leave the horses farther out until we turn in, then bring them in close. That way we save some grass for them. Besides, if your enemy kills your horse, he doesn't need to kill you. A man afoot in these plains is as good as dead."

"Shouldn't we take turns standing guard?" Dub asked.

"My horse is an excellent sentry after dark. And whoever's watching us is keeping their distance, and without a fire they won't know where we are."

"Mr. Fargo," Nate said, "why are men watching you?"

"And shooting at you," Nate added.

"Well, you boys have a right to know."

Fargo reminded them about the brutal attack on the Quakers yesterday, and added the detail about the mysterious doeskin pouch the old matriarch had given him.

"The yellow-bellied sons of bitches," Dub said. "But what's in that pouch that they want it so bad?"

"That's a poser, all right. For that matter, you can rob unarmed people without killing them. But I'll tell you this much— when border ruffians don't bother to steal from their victims, that tells me they're getting good money from somebody who's got deep pockets."

"F'rinstance, who?"

Fargo shifted his back against a rough cottonwood, scratching himself like a buffalo. "Boys, to you this land looks empty.

But I've marked the changes over the years. The Philadelphia lawyers, the New York land hunters, the deep-rock miners, the railroad barons—they've got their own 'scouts,' and they're out here right now, figuring out how they can divide the West up among them and then tax the rest of us to guarantee their fortunes. It's all percentages and angles. And sometimes these scouts have to stir up some disasters to further their cause. They don't care a frog's fat ass for the natural beauty or for whoever they have to destroy to do their masters' bidding."

"Damn," Dub remarked. "Our pa use to talk a lot like that. Anyhow, can't you just open that pouch?"

"The order from that dying messenger," Fargo said, "was to leave it sealed and give it to an officer. Even though I'm not a soldier, I just signed a contract for more work with the frontier outposts. That puts me under military law."

"Oh. Then how's come you don't just take it to the nearest fort? There's Fort Hays a few days northeast of here."

Fargo grinned. Young men never seemed to run dry of questions.

"Because," he said, "as you saw yesterday, those heel flies pestering me will kill me. They're staying on me like ugly on a buzzard. Long as I stay in this area, they'll try to kill me with some discretion. But if I make a beeline out of here, I'll have every jayhawker in the territory trying to snuff my wick. You two sharpshooters need to think about all that before you decide to stick or quit."

"I'll stick," Dub said immediately.

"Me, too," Nate echoed. "Pa always said even God hates a coward."

Fargo rolled into his blankets. "Judging from the quality of your mother, and your marksmanship, your pa was quite a man."

"Top of the heap," Dub said proudly. "How 'bout your folks, Mr. Fargo?"

"Best get some shut-eye," Fargo told them. "Could be a long day tomorrow."

Fargo shook the McCallister boys awake at first light, then whistled in the Ovaro and tacked him.

"We'll skip morning grub and grab something at Sublette," he explained. "From here on in, keep your eyes peeled."

Sublette was about a three-hour ride. Before he hit leather, Fargo lay flat on the ground and placed his right ear just above it.

"Ain't you s'pose to press your ear to the ground?" Dub asked.

"No, just above it, or all you'll hear is your own heart pulsing. Well, no big group of riders closing in, anyhow. Let's dust our hocks."

All three riders scanned the wide-open plains as they rode. The bloodred sun rose higher and turned a burning yellow.

"Mr. Fargo?" Dub said. "I been using my eyes like you said to yesterday. I think there's riders way to the south, tracking us."

"Good man," Fargo praised. "I see them, too."

When Nate started to guzzle water from his canteen, Fargo spoke up. "Gradual on that."

"Why? Water ain't scarce in these parts."

"When you drink water in the sun, you just sweat it out and don't get the use of it. And both you jays, stop pulling your horses' heads up when they're smelling the ground. All horses do that in country they're not familiar with. It calms them down."

"Dang," Nate said. "Riding with you, Mr. Fargo, is like being in school."

"Yeah, except this is school for staying alive. And you better remember your lessons."

"Yessir, schoolmaster."

A half hour later they topped a limestone ridge and saw Sublette lying in a bowl-shaped depression below them. The place had grown since Fargo's first time there awhile back. The big, split-log trading post sat beside a feeder creek of the Cimarron. But a sprawl of newer structures—and a few large tents—had grown up around it like spokes around a hub. The Quakers Fargo had guided in two days earlier, after dark, were camped with other pilgrims in good graze about a quarter mile east of the trading post.

Fargo drew his Colt and palmed the wheel to check his loads.

"All right, boys," he said. "Whoever's watching us knows we're riding in, and I've seen some mirror signals. Keep your weapons close to hand. Here's how we play it. I ride in front. Nate rides about twenty paces behind me and keeps his eyes on both flanks. Dub, you're rearguard about twenty paces behind your bother. Keep looking behind us."

Fargo holstered his short iron. "If anybody draws a bead on any of us, plug him. But stay frosty—everybody is likely armed down there, and we don't want to kill a man just because he shifts his rifle. Savvy that?"

Both boys nodded, looking nervous but determined. As they rode in along a rutted trail, Fargo realized the lone trading post had evolved into a rough-and-tumble settlement. *Very* rough: there were no raw-lumber boardwalks, no jailhouse, no hotel, no church or school, no tie-rails even. Chinese vendors in floppy blue blouses pushed wooden carts, hawking buffalo tongues pickled in brine, honeycombs, and sacks of ginger snaps.

Fargo, who had wandered nearly every trail in the West, recognized a few of the hostile faces watching them ride in, but nobody he'd buy a drink for.

"Hell and damnation!" Nate said. "Is this Sodom or Gomorrah, Mr. Fargo?"

"Never mind the gawking. Just consider it a hellhole filled with enemies. This is a good time to keep your mouth shut and your eyes open."

Fargo spotted a crude sign that said SALOON AND EATS. No frame building with slatted bat wings here, just a large tent with three sides and an open front. Inside, men stood at narrow counters, eating and drinking.

"Let's stoke our bellies before we hit the trading post," he said. "At least it'll be easy to see our horses."

The three men reined in, swung down, and hobbled their mounts. The interior was a thick blue haze of smoke. Some men pretended to ignore them, others aimed hostile stares.

"It makes no sense," Fargo muttered to his companions. "It's like they have a score to settle."

Fargo spotted a bunch of buffalo hiders in their characteristic bloodstained, greasy rags. "Stop staring at them, Nate," he warned. "Hiders are a rough crowd, especially when they see a man ride in on a farm nag."

The only item on the menu was beef and biscuits, so Fargo ordered three plates.

"Fresh out," replied a balding barkeep in sleeve garters and a string tie.

Fargo could see the Chinese cook behind him, stirring a pot. The Trailsman knew this was a make or break moment: these frontier vermin were listening to every word, and if Fargo didn't crack the whip now, he and the brothers might not make it out alive.

"Lissenup, you dough-belly peckerwood, and lissenup good: I don't chew my cabbage twice. Now, you rustle up that grub pronto or I'll wear your guts for garters."

The barkeep paled. Fargo watched his eyes slant toward the left side of the tent. A heavyset thug, whose hand-tooled holster was tied down with a rawhide whang, shook his head no.

Without hesitation, Fargo pushed his way over and confronted the man. Fargo rested his palm on the butt of his Colt.

"Who in the hell are you to decide if I eat or not, cockchafer?" he demanded.

"Fuck you, buckskins. You ain't—"

Fargo backhanded him so hard that the man staggered backward. He cursed, his right hand twitching toward his big dragoon pistol.

Quicker than eyesight Fargo's Colt leaped into his fist. "Don't miscalculate yourself, mister. You're about one eyeblink away from crossing the River Jordan. Now toss down that hog leg and light a shuck out of here before I ventilate your guts."

Suddenly losing his bravado, the thug did as ordered. This time, when Fargo returned to the crude plank bar, no one met his eye. And three plates of steaming food were waiting.

"Damn, Mr. Fargo," Dub said, "you sure put the shawl on that son of a bitch. But how's come everybody around here acts like you raped their mothers?"

Fargo sopped up some pot liquor with a biscuit. "I'm hanged if I know, boy. But I got a feeling we'll find out quick enough."

"Three beers," Fargo ordered when the trio had finished eating. "And draw 'em nappy."

The bartender pretended not to hear. Fargo had just made his point with the thug, and didn't want to overplay his hand. So this time his tone was less threatening.

"You best clean your ears, bottles. I ordered three beers. I don't care who told you to give me the frosty mitt—you've got more to fear from me than from him."

The nervous barkeep met his eye. "I b'lieve that's so, stranger. Three barley pops it is, nappy."

"Can't we have whiskey?" Dub complained in a low voice.

"Pipe down, you jay. The whiskey, in roach pits like this, doubles as undertaker's fluid."

"Yeah, but me and Nate ain't never—"

"Just enjoy your beer and keep your eyes to all sides. Case you haven't noticed, there's draw-shoot killers in this bunch. And they're on the featheredge of shooting us to trap bait."

The mugs of beer came, and Fargo was surprised to find it cold—somebody around here must have harvested winter ice and stored it in a sawdust pit. He laid some coins on the counter.

"On the house," the barkeep said. "I got a feeling I've been misinformed about you."

"How so?"

The barkeep shook his head. "Rather not say. It could have consequences for me, if you take my drift. But it wouldn't be the first slander spread around here."

The barkeep was obviously scared and Fargo didn't push it. Just then he recognized the Ovaro's trouble whicker and glanced outside. A furtive-looking man with a soup-strainer mustache stood between Fargo's pinto and Nate's big dobbin.

The moment he reached for the offside saddlebag, Fargo cleared leather and shot him through the hand. The would-be thief howled and took off on foot. In a heartbeat, Dub and Nate bolted from the tent saloon and tackled him. Fargo followed them into the filthy street.

"Jesus Christ, mister, you shot my goddamn hand!" the man howled.

"That's because I knew you weren't stealing my horse," Fargo replied. "Or I'd've shot your noggin. What are you after in my saddle pockets?"

"Not a damn thing. I was just admiring your fine pinto."

"Admire a cat's tail, you lying bastard. Tell me, is your boss a border ruffian, or does he just pay them to do his dirt work?"

"Mister, you're fishing in the wrong pond. I got no boss."

Fargo's face hardened until it looked chiseled in granite. "Don't piss down my back and tell me it's raining. Now talk out."

"Look, I'll tell you the straight—I was tryin' to get into your saddlebag. I just wanted food, is all."

"You look well fed to me."

"Mister, my hand hurts to beat hell. Let me go or kill me."

Fargo didn't like the attention they were getting from inside, nor their vulnerable position in the street.

"Let him up, boys. We'll get to the bottom of this. Dub, that's a Colt Navy he's toting. Empty the wheel—you can use the bullets."

"Katy Christ, Mr. Fargo," Dub said after the man hurried off. "How's come you got so many enemies around here?"

"Damned if I know," Fargo admitted. "Why am I so handsome? I can tell you this much: I've yet to meet one man in Sublette I'd trust to hold my horse."

Fargo and the McCallister boys rode to the big log trading post, the only structure in the settlement with a tie rail and water trough out front. Fargo loosened the Ovaro's girth and dropped the bridle so the stallion could drink.

"Those big horses of yours," he told the brothers, "will be perfect for hauling the goods back to your farm. Make sure you get gunnysacks you can tie off."

The interior of the building was a strange combination of smells: new leather, harsh tobacco, male sweat, and the salt tang of cured meat. A space had been cleared just inside the door for a faro game now in progress. At least a dozen men sat on nail kegs and vegetable cans, eyes glued to the female case tender.

Fargo did a double take himself. The lovely Mexican-Indian girl had copper-tinted skin and high, pronounced cheekbones. Her white peasant blouse bared both slim shoulders and a generous glimpse of full breasts like rising loaves.

Nate spoke up too loudly, and every head turned in their direction. "Is that poker they're playing, Mr. Fargo?"

The room erupted in contemptuous laughter.

"No, mooncalf," barbed a man in filthy fringed buckskins. "It's tiddlywinks."

"The kid's fresh off the tit," joined in someone else. "Don't even know gee from haw."

Nate blushed crimson to his earlobes. "The hell'd I say?" he muttered to Fargo.

Fargo was on the verge of slapping the kid. It was hard to inspire fear in your enemies, he realized, when you were sided by ignorant shave-tails.

"Just keep your lips sewed shut in places like this," he muttered back. "That's a faro game, not poker. No man ignorant of cards need bother going west. It's as bad as not being able to handle a horse."

"Will you teach us cards?" Dub asked.

"Yeah, if you rubes don't get me killed first. Christ, you two stick out like a Kansas City fire engine."

"Ain't our fault we're young," Dub said.

Fargo grinned. "A good point, and I'm caught upon it."

Fargo noticed something odd. The men were staring daggers at him just like the men in the saloon had. But the fetching girl couldn't make it much more obvious that she approved of the new arrival. Never taking her smoldering dark eyes off him, she pulled one side of her blouse down an inch or so lower, revealing a chocolate-colored glimpse of the ring around her nipple.

"Say . . . look at the cat heads on her," Dub whispered. "It ain't me and Nate she's looking at. I think she likes you, Mr. Fargo."

"I wonder," Fargo said absently. He was used to instant attention from women, but not usually anything quite this brazen in front of a crowd.

"Hey, Skye! The hell you doin' in these diggings?"

Fargo spotted a burly, full-bearded man in a long gray duster turning away from the front counter. He held two boxes of factory-pressed cartridges.

"Old Jules!" Fargo greeted his friend and one-time scouting partner. "Still above the horizon, I see."

"Shit, an act of God can't kill this old hoss! I can drink more rotgut, screw more women, and kill more grizzlies with my bare hands than any swingin' dick on the continent!"

Old Jules shifted his glance to the boys. "The hell's on the spit? You corruptin' children now?"

Fargo definitely didn't like all the hostile stares. "Boys," he muttered to the brothers, "go stock up with the money your ma gave you. Meet me outside."

Fargo sent a high sign to Old Jules, who followed him outside.

"The hell you doin' this far south?" Old Jules demanded. "I heard tell you was up in the Nebraska Panhandle."

"You might say I was delayed."

Old Jules avoided his eyes after this remark, digging at a tick in his beard. "Uh-huh. That's what I hear."

"The hell's that s'pose to mean?"

"Ahh . . ." The old scout drew out a flask from underneath his duster. "Cut the dust?"

"Nix on that. I want to know what you've heard."

Old Jules swallowed a jolt and grimaced. "Damn! That panther piss could raise blood blisters on new leather."

"Give, Jules."

"Let's just say I don't believe a word I've heard. Matter fact, if I did, I'd a shot you on sight like a mad dog. But 'pears like everybody around here is banking yaller boys—and they'll do any damn thing to earn 'em 'cept honest work."

"All right, you're creeping closer. Now if you wander near a point, feel free to make it."

"Here's the long and short of it, Skye. They's a rumor around here 'bout how you dressed in butternut and led some jayhawkers or pukes—which bunch ain't clear—in an attack on some Quakers. Then, or so they say, you changed back into your reg'lar duds and pretended to help the Quakers so's you'd look innocent. It's all horseshit, but that's the story."

"So that's the way of it," Fargo said quietly. "Who started peddling this rumor?"

Old Jules shrugged his massive shoulders. "Hell, what comes after what's next? I just rode in this mornin' to stock up on ammo, hoss. I signed a contract with Overland to guide a caravan down the Santa Fe Trail. I'm headin' out right now to meet them at Raton Pass."

"Tell me," Fargo said, "have you ever heard of border ruffians this far west?"

"Don't make no sense. Their dicker is a border skirmish twixt the pro-slavers in Missouri and the abolitionists in the Kansas Territory. 'Course, that's mostly just lip deep—both bunches ain't nothin' but graveyard rats and don't care a jackstraw 'bout the coloreds. Still, this is a far piece west to ride when there ain't hardly anybody to rob."

"Yeah, well, that's another stumper," Fargo said. "Jules, I watched that attack on the Quakers, and the border riders hardly even bothered to steal anything. You ever heard of them passing up loot?"

"Yeah, in a pig's ass. Them butternuts would steal a dead fly from a blind spider."

Fargo nodded. "So what was the point? I'd say they were paid to mount that raid. But why?"

Old Jules removed a plug of chewing tobacco from his pocket and sliced off a chaw with a small clasp knife. When he had it cheeked and juicing good, he spat an amber stream into the grass.

"It's too far north for me, Skye," he finally replied. "But I got more bad news. When you was at Fort Leavenworth, do you 'member hearin' 'bout General Hoffman and that blowhard senator?"

Fargo nodded. Brigadier General Daniel Hoffman, and an escort of twelve crack soldiers, were to accompany Missouri Senator James Drummond on a fact-finding mission for the Kansas-Pacific Railroad's proposed transcontinental route. Drummond was a notorious "katydid booster," adept at gaining federal money for projects out West.

"Well, the same jaspers spreadin' the lies about you claim the entire party has dropped off the earth," Jules explained. "No mirror signals for a week now."

"Let me guess," Fargo put in. "I led an attack on them."

Jules nodded. "Ain't it the drizzlin' shits? That's what some around here are sayin'."

Fargo began to feel the first glimmers of enlightenment. "Why didn't I grab hold of that sooner? Jules, that proposed K-P route is just north of here."

Old Jules nodded. "You got a better think piece than me, Skye. I still can't read the sign—can't even *find* it."

"Me either, but I'll work this trail out. Jules, I see some of the butternuts around Sublette. I suspect some others are wearing regular clothes to disguise their motives. Are they camped near here?"

"Hell, they must me, but I can't tell you where. I steer wide of them sons of bitches."

Just then Dub and Nate staggered out of the trading post loaded down with gunnysacks filled with supplies.

"Boys," Fargo said, "haul that stuff back to your ma and Krissy."

"You ain't coming?" Dub asked.

Fargo shook his head. "I got work to do around here, and I

best do it quick. Besides, why should you two get the crappy end of the stick? I'm the one they're after. You boys should be safe riding home, but keep your guns to hand, and remember everything I taught you on the trail."

"Hell, we was hoping to side you," Nate said. "We like the crappy end of the stick."

"You still feel that way after everything you've seen here?"

"More than ever," Dub said. "Pa taught us it's better to die for a just cause than to live for nothing."

Old Jules chuckled. "Hell, these tads is game, Skye. Swear 'em in."

"And we proved to you that we can shoot," Nate added.

"For a fact you can, and I admit I'll need help—I see that now. Come on back, but don't ride into the settlement. Pitch a cold camp along the creek east of Sublette. I'll find you."

Dub flashed his gap-toothed grin. "Maybe 'work' ain't all you got to do around here." He handed Fargo a folded sheet of foolscap. "That pretty gal with the nice thing-a-ma-bobs asked me to give you this."

Fargo unfolded it and frowned at the rough spelling. Haltingly, he read it out loud, " 'Meet me just after dark at the cottonwood grove north of the trading post.' " It was signed, "Rosario."

"Fargo, you always was one to be combin' pussy hair out of your teeth," Old Jules roweled him. "Good-lookin' wimmin flock to you like flies to syrup, you fortune-kissed son of a bitch."

But Fargo's frown deepened until there was a crease between his eyebrows. "All that glitters is not gold, Jules. This gal Rosario has got something on her mind besides a quick poke."

# 6

Old Jules rode out of Sublette soon after the McCallister boys, and Fargo found himself alone in a rough and dangerous settlement—a place crawling with scurvy-ridden toughs eager to kill him.

Nonetheless, he had no plans to lie low. He had learned, from hard experience, to take trouble by the horns. If a man cringed in the shadows his enemies were emboldened. So he moved about the place freely and openly, letting no man stare him down.

Not everyone, he soon noticed, seemed hostile toward him. Several men greeted him cheerfully, and Fargo supposed they had either not heard the rumors about him or didn't know who he was. Or, perhaps even better, they set no store by the lies because they mistrusted the source. Who that mysterious source was had become the hard nub of Fargo's problem, but getting information out of the locals was proving harder than finding ducks in the desert.

At the east end of the rough settlement Fargo spotted an open-fronted shed with a shingle advertising haircuts, tooth extraction, and hot baths. Hobbling the Ovaro right out front in plain sight, he started inside.

"Need a tooth pulled, mister?" said a high-voiced man who was all of five feet tall. He was busy shooing off flies with a feather swisher. "Only two dollars, and I use laudanum."

"Just a hot bath," Fargo said, removing his hat and whipping the dust off it.

"Yessir. Cost you four bits, soap and towel included."

While the diminutive man poured hot water into a wooden tub, Fargo pulled off his shirt.

"Land love us!" the proprietor exclaimed, staring at Fargo's muscle-ridged torso. "Those are bullet holes and knife scars, ain't they?"

"Mostly. That pretty purple one in the middle was made by a Cheyenne lance point."

"I've given quite a few men scars myself," the man boasted. "That's why I had to scratch 'shaves' off my sign."

Fargo laughed, eyes cutting out front to check on his horse.

"Say," the man said in his near-feminine voice. "I know you! You're Mr. Skye Fargo. The hombre they call the Trailsman. I'm Dusty Jones."

Fargo unbuckled his shell belt and draped it over the edge of the tub. "Pleased to meetcha, Dusty. I take it you've heard about my 'massacre,' too?"

"That's a load of whale snot. Mr. Fargo, when you talk like a girl and stand knee-high to a burro, like I do, you ain't welcome among men. And when you ain't welcome, you think for yourself. No, I first heard of you five, six years ago. In a story in the *New York Herald* by a Miss—Miss—"

"McKenna," Fargo supplied, his lips twitching into a smile as he remembered her. "Beautiful woman."

"Sure, that's her name. This lady wrote a sockdologer of a story about how you saved her and a bunch of orphans out in the Dakota land. That lady called you a 'knight in buckskins.'"

Fargo looked embarrassed. "Yeah, well, she can really slather it on."

"Maybe so, but a knight in buckskins don't attack defenseless people."

Fargo finished stripping and eased into the hot water. "'Preciate that, Dusty. But tell me—who do you think got that massacre story started?"

"Likely one of the border ruffians, to put the blame off them. Except they like to be called 'Butternut Guerrillas.'"

"Yeah, and I prefer John the Baptist." Fargo sudsed his hair and beard with strong lye soap. "Any idea who leads this local bunch?"

"Mr. Fargo, that gang is one pile of turds I try not to step into. There's one fellow with an eye patch, seems to swagger it around and give orders. Don't know his name. And there's some big bastard with long hair tied off in a knot—he seems to be some kind of topkick."

The Ovaro snorted, and Fargo swiped soap from his eyes, drawing his Colt. But it was only a curious old hound, sniffing at the pinto.

"Any idea where they camp?" Fargo asked.

"No, sir, I'd sooner know the entrance to hell. But they stay somewhere close because they come and go freely."

Fargo finished his bath, dried off with a scrap of rough towel, and dressed. The little man gave him a quick brushing with a whisk broom.

"Thanks, Dusty," Fargo said, slipping him a silver dollar. "Keep the change."

"Thanks, Mr. Fargo. I won't part with this one—you touched it, so it must be lucky."

"Lucky? If I was you," Fargo advised as he headed out the front of the shed, "I'd spend the damn thing mighty quick."

The afternoon sun was throwing long shadows, and Fargo had an unpleasant duty before keeping his tryst with the pretty mixed-breed Rosario—first came a visit to the Quaker camp.

He trotted the stallion next to the creek, making sure his Henry was loosened in its saddle scabbard. An ambush could come at any moment, and in his present mood he welcomed the possibility. He considered the border ruffians among the lowest trash on the frontier, and anytime they chose to open the ball, he was ready to waltz.

The Quaker women and children had camped at an elbow bend in the creek. As Fargo rode up, their mistrustful, fearful glances stabbed at his guts. Obviously they, too, had heard from Dame Rumor.

He found Esther Emmerick stirring a three-legged cooking pot over a campfire. The unwelcome glance she gave him persuaded Fargo to remain in the saddle.

"Mrs. Emmerick." He touched the brim of his hat. "How you folks getting on?"

"We're surviving, Lord willing."

"Have you made any plans yet?"

"If we have, Mr. Fargo, we certainly won't disclose them to thee."

"I see. So your religion allows you to hate a man on the basis of a fake rumor?"

"I did not say I hate thee."

"Mrs. Emmerick, look at me."

Reluctantly, she did so.

"Do you honest-to-God believe that I led that raid?"

"The Friends do not take oaths on the Lord's name."

"All right," Fargo said, "do you really believe it?"

Esther studied him closely. "I see a gun on thy hip, another in thy saddle, and a knife in thy boot. Thou are a man who consorts with violence constantly."

"Yes, ma'am, all true. But you're taking the long way around the barn. Do you believe I led that raid?"

This time her tired, suffering eyes studied only his face.

"No," she finally replied, her face softening. "Thou are a tough, sometimes even hard, man who has surely killed many souls. But thou are no murderer—I see the decency and kindness in thine eyes."

"Well, you're right that I'm no murderer. I'll settle for that. I know you folks set no store by vengeance, but I mean to get to the bottom of this."

"As thou said, Mr. Fargo, the Friends are not vindictive. We will turn the other cheek."

"Fine, but I won't. If murderers go unchecked, no one will be safe. There's no law out here yet, and soldiers are stretched way too thin."

She shook her head. "Vigilantes are not the answer."

"They are when there's no one else. You know, last I heard, the Old Testament was still part of the Bible. 'An eye for an eye, a tooth for a tooth.' Anyhow, let's not butt heads over it. Do you feel safe here?"

"The men around here are mostly riffraff," she replied, "but they're leaving us in peace—for now. We have hired a guide and will be returning to Pennsylvania as soon as he has purchased supplies."

Fargo nodded. "Good. This is no country for peaceful people—not yet, anyhow."

"There we can agree, young man. But our men—or at least their bodies—will dwell on these lonely plains forever, their grave unmarked."

Fargo knew better. That grave had been shallow, and by now predators and buzzards—or perhaps even roving Indians—had exposed, even mutilated, the bodies. They would end up above-ground as piles of bleached bones, the skulls turned into castles for worms and beetles. But he kept that grisly thought to himself and simply bade Esther farewell.

As Fargo rode back toward the trading post, the problem of his rendezvous with Rosario began niggling at him again.

Her purpose eluded him. He had always found the game of seduction easy, but rarely had a woman offered the favor of her body upon first glance at him—and without learning his name or at least exchanging a word of conversation.

From the beginning he had suspected a trap of some kind, one meant to send Skye Fargo to his ancestors. But how deeply involved was the girl? Why she would even be in a death trap like Sublette was a mystery. Was she a willing participant in this plot, or being strong-armed by the jayhawkers—as women out West often were?

"Orphans and bachelors preferred," Fargo muttered grimly. "No Quakers need apply."

He still had about an hour before the sun went down, and Fargo felt a stirring of hunger. He flagged down a street vendor and purchased a few roast beef sandwiches wrapped in cheese-cloth. He ate one as he headed north from the trading post. The longhorn beef was tough as shoe leather and full of gristle, and the bread stale, but he choked it down with plenty of water.

In the gathering dusk he could see a big cottonwood grove about a half mile ahead, the one Rosario must have meant. He was still a little early, so Fargo reined in and stood up in the stir-rups, searching all around him. He could spot no tails, nor any sign of the girl. Which must mean everyone was already waiting in the grove—the trap was set.

A bloodred sun blazed for a final moment in the west, then seemed to be swallowed by the endless blue-black plains. Fargo swung down and tethered the Ovaro in the lush graze. Then he un-tied the cantle straps and unrolled his blanket, wrapping it around his head.

He waited perhaps twenty minutes, letting his eyes adjust to total darkness. When he removed the blanket, his night vision was remarkably sharp—as he rode closer to the grove, he could make out separate limbs and see well back into the trees.

Fargo rode slowly around the grove, eyes slanted downward. In the silvery moonlight, he found signs of two riders. He knew they had been here recently because the crushed grass had barely begun to spring back up.

After a minute or two spent following the trail, Fargo came across two horses hobbled near a rill just past the grove. He moved the Ovaro into the concealment of the trees, then returned to the hobbled mounts.

"Hee—" he said in a harsh whisper, slapping one of the mounts on its glossy rump. "Hee—"

Both horses nickered frantically, and Fargo faded back, kneeling in the tall grass. Moments later two thugs, short guns to hand, burst from the trees.

"What is it, Harney?" a nervous voice demanded. "See anybody?"

"Ahh, it's prolly just a snake that spooked 'em," Harney retorted.

"No, it's snakes that *ride* 'em," Fargo called out, standing up in the moonlight. "Look dead ahead, puke pails."

Fargo could have killed both of them from hiding, for cause, but it was his way to give enemies a fighting chance when the numbers weren't too great against him. And they both took that chance, spotting his shadowy form and starting to blast wildly away. In contrast, even as orange spear tips of flame spat from their muzzles and bullets snapped past him, Fargo took deliberate aim.

His first shot spun the man on the left halfway around, and he crumpled screaming. Fargo dropped the second one like a sack of salt. He moved in rapidly and found the screaming man wheezing like a leaky bellows, suffering from a lung shot. Fargo saved a bullet, sliding the Arkansas toothpick from his boot and opening the man's throat wide to finish him off. He wiped the blade off on his enemy's pants leg.

The ambusher on the right had died instantly, his heart ripped open. Fargo took a closer look. As he'd expected, both men wore the butternut-dyed homespun of border ruffians. The one on the left was large and mallet-fisted and—even in death—wore the perpetual sneer of a saloon bully. The other one was an ugly cur with a pockmarked face. Neither man fit the descriptions Old Jules and Dusty Jones had given him.

**45**

"Rosario," he called out. "It's Skye Fargo."

"Yes, I am here."

Guided by the sound of her frightened voice, Fargo joined her near the center of the grove. She sat on a log in a splash of moonlight, a lace mantilla wrapping her shoulders.

She greeted his arrival.

"Both dead," he assured her. "That's two plug-uglies that will do no more raping and killing. How much did they pay you?"

Even in the moonlight he saw her nostrils flare in anger. "Me? You are loco, Fargo. I am rich already from the faro game. My—how do you say?—'payment' was that I would not be killed if I did as I was told."

"I find that easy to believe," Fargo said. "And I always give a woman on the frontier the benefit of the doubt. Now, who forced you to do this?"

"*No puedo decir.*"

"Yes, you *can* say."

Fargo sat on the log beside her. "I've just about had a belly-ful around here, lady. Now give it to me straight."

Her dark, almond-shaped eyes glimmered like foxfire in the moonlight. A scent of gardenia perfume teased Fargo's nostrils. "Or you will do what? Kill me?"

"Don't be a fool."

"Rape me?"

"I never steal what's freely offered. And I get plenty offered."

Her lips twisted in a sneer. "And, I will offer like all the others?"

"I sure hope so. But dessert comes after the meal, and right now I'm hungry for hard facts."

"Never have I known such a—confident man."

"You might call me . . . cocksure," Fargo quipped.

"Cocksure? What does this mean, cocksure?"

Fargo wisely let it go. "Look, Rosario, I need answers. Who put you up to this?"

"His name is Moss. He comes in for the faro, and that is what his filthy friends call him. He wears a—how do you say?—over one eye . . . ?"

"Eye patch?"

"Exactly. He said he would let all his men rape me, and then he would kill me, if I did not trick you out here."

"Moss what?"

She shook her head. "I do not know. But he is a leader among the pigs who keep this place in terror. So is another called . . . Chanhai, I think."

Fargo felt the hair on his nape stiffen. "Do you mean Shanghai?"

"You know him?"

"I know of him. Shanghai Webb. He led a scalper army in Mexico. Killed hundreds of women and children and sold their scalps for bounties in Chihuahua."

"Yes, he has the look of a butcher."

"But he is not the leader, right?"

"I think there is another man above him. But unlike his—his *braceros*, he does not show himself. I think he is afraid to be . . ."

"Recognized?"

She nodded. "I think he is."

"Yeah, I think so, too. Do you know where they camp?"

"No, and I do not wish to know. Anyone who looks for it will find his own grave."

Fargo said, "What is a woman like you doing here?"

"I was a gambler's woman. He lost much money to the men who own the trading post. He gave them me in trade for the money. They are honest men and do not use me as a whore. Instead, I run the faro game, and we all make money."

"I saw why the moment I walked in today. Those men were there to look at you, not to make money."

He felt her hand on his arm. "And you, Trailsman? What are you doing here?"

"Right now I'm chopping wood and letting the chips fall where they may."

"I do not understand."

"Do you understand this?"

Fargo pulled her into his strong arms and crushed her lips with his, both their tongues exploring hungrily.

"Yes, I understand," she whispered breathlessly, panting like an overheated animal. "But teach me more."

Glad to oblige, Fargo dropped his gun belt and pulled her down into the grass, tugging her long skirt up around her hips. She was naked beneath it, and the moonlight limned her supple thighs, gently curved stomach, and a thick, dark bush. He pulled

**47**

her lace shawl aside and tugged up the peasant blouse to expose her firm globes with their hard, dark nipples that formed hard points. He licked both of them stiff while she moaned encouragement.

"Most men ignore those, Skye Fargo, in their greedy lust for the hole. But you know how to treat them."

Her eager hands untied his fly and released his straining manhood. Fargo felt a hot tickle of pleasure when she stroked it, drawing a sharp breath of astonishment.

"I thought only a stallion could have one like this! Mount me, stallion! Mount me now!"

She scissored her legs wide for him, and Fargo nudged the swollen head of his shaft past the chamois-soft folds of her nether portal. Rosario was hot and slippery, and he parted the pliant walls of her sex in a long thrust that made both of them groan.

Her fingernails clawed into his buttocks as Fargo rammed into her over and over, faster and faster, harder and harder, each thrust moving both of them across the grass.

"Ayyy!" she cried out as rapid climaxes shook her. *"Ayyy, eso, sí!"* Fargo lost all control of his muscles as he reached his own release, a finish so powerful and spectacular that both lay dazed for uncounted minutes, awareness returning only slowly as if they were floating to the surface of a deep pool.

Finally: "Fargo," she said weakly, "I see why you are so . . . cocksure. This was worth dying for."

Fargo started dressing. "The hell kind of fool talk is that?"

"Do you think they will let me live now? With two of their fellow pigs slaughtered? They will think I warned you."

"Yeah, I've thought about that."

Without warning, Fargo's right fist shot out and punched her on those beautiful lips—not hard enough to damage her teeth, just to cut both lips open. He followed up immediately with a backhand to her right eye.

"I hated like hell to do that, Rosario. But you understand why I had to?"

"To save my life. Now they will think you beat me for leading you into a trap from which you escaped."

"Sure. By the time you walk back, you'll have a hell of a shiner. And don't wipe off the blood—it'll look worse when it dries. Where do you stay?"

"I have a room at the trading post."

"You better take off—they may start wondering where their men are."

"Fargo? We will do this again? It will be in my thoughts every day."

He grinned. "And in mine every night. You're a beautiful woman. But no way can we meet if it risks your life. We'll have to see which way the wind sets. Now go home before they catch us."

Rosario disappeared into the shroud of night, and Fargo turned to one last item of business. He returned to the two dead bodies and wrestled off their shell belts and handguns, both Remington single-action repeaters. He draped them around his neck and moved out to their horses, which had calmed down by now.

He checked both saddle scabbards. The first weapon was a good find: a seven-shot U.S. Cavalry carbine, .56 caliber, with a bandolier of ammo. The other was an inferior, .32 caliber single-shot rifle widely known as a British trade gun because they were sold or traded to Indians before British trappers were driven out.

Fargo took it anyway, knowing the McCallister boys could split a sunbeam with a blunderbuss. Firepower, and as much as possible, would be the only defense when the jayhawkers made their inevitable massed attack.

Fargo nudged the rifles under his cantle straps, then lugged each body out to a horse and lashed them on with the ropes coiled around the saddle horns. He untied the hobbles, turned each horse west, and smacked it on the rump. He knew they'd run straight for the corral, especially with weight on their backs.

He considered following them, but thought better of it. Locating the border ruffians was not a problem—finding them without being killed, on the other hand, was.

He recalled Rosario's words when he asked her if she knew where they camped: *Anyone who looks for it will find his own grave.*

# 7

Rafe Belloch, Shanghai Webb, Moss Harper, and Jake Ketchum met inside Belloch's headquarters in the dugout. The mood was tense. Only fifteen minutes earlier two horses had returned carrying their dead riders.

"I guess the plan with Rosario didn't pan out," Moss said.

Rafe gave a sarcastic bark. In the coal-oil lantern light his eyes were like hard, flat chips of flint. "Good God, strike a light! Call this man Sir Oracle!"

"The hell's that mean?" Moss demanded. "More of your high-hatted talk?"

"Take the cob out of your sitter. It's just a manner of speaking."

Rafe interlaced his fingers behind his back and paced the length of the partially submerged structure.

"Shanghai," he said, "I told you to put good men on this job."

"Hell, boss, Les and Harney are—good men. They rode with me in Mexico. They both snuck into a Texas Ranger camp outside San Antonio and killed four of 'em in their sleep."

"I see. Well, evidently Fargo was awake. And I suppose you put a good sneak thief on the job of stealing that pouch, eh? The stupid stumblebum comes back with a hole shot through his hand."

"Shanghai," Moss said, "you ain't thinking, are you, that maybe that half-breed bitch hornswoggled us? She's part Mexer, and you know how sly them Mexer women can be."

"Not likely. I crossed paths with her when she was returning to the trading post. Fargo beat hell out of her—her face was a mess."

Rafe abruptly stopped pacing and looked at Shanghai. "Beat her, you say?"

"Worked her over pretty good."

"That doesn't comport with what I've heard about Fargo."

"Comport?" Jake repeated. "The hell's that mean?"

"I'm not your damn schoolmaster," Rafe snapped.

"Maybe you heard wrong about him," Moss told his employer. "I'd *gut* any bitch that lured me into a trap like that."

Rafe mulled that and nodded. "I don't know the man personally, so perhaps you're right. But, gents, there's an old saying: 'the cause is secret, but the effect is known.' And the *effect* was on the men—half of them saw those horses ride in. Morale is everything in a fight like this."

"Well," Shanghai reminded him, "won't be long before that report you wrote about him will spread through the Territory."

"We can't count on that now. It could be weeks before soldiers react, but Fargo is taking the bit in his teeth. Trust me, gents. I may seem like a skinny dandy to you, but I read men like scholars read books. Fargo is the kind of man who gets twenty miles down the road while others are debating whether to leave today or tomorrow."

"All due respect, boss," Shanghai said, "but you're building a pimple into a peak. Sure, he's got a set of stones on him, I grant that. But there's a chink in his armor somewhere, and when we find it we'll pound away at it."

This seemed to mollify Belloch somewhat. He nodded approval. "I like that attitude, Shanghai. But be very careful, boys, all of you. Most of you grew up east of the Big Muddy. But Fargo's reputation was carved out beyond the fringes of civilization. This is his back forty, so to speak, and like any good farmer, he knows every inch of his land."

Jake looked perplexed. "Fargo owns land? Where?"

"Jesus Christ with a wooden dick!" Moss exclaimed. "Jake, if brains was horseshit, you'd have a clean corral."

Rafe waved this aside impatiently. "No more halfway measures. Tomorrow we start flushing that crusading bastard out. The word on Senator Drummond and General Hoffman must be getting out by now. I want Fargo cold as a basement floor before he can deliver that pouch."

"Hell," Shanghai said, "you're getting ahead of the roundup, ain'tcha, boss? We don't even know what's in that pouch."

"We know what may be in it, and that's danger enough. Even

this far west we have some limitations—one of them is murdering a senator."

Again Rafe stopped pacing. Unexpectedly, a confident smile touched his thin, expressive lips. "So far his clover has been deep. But the worm will turn, boys. Mark me on that."

After sending the two dead border ruffians back to their outlaw camp, Fargo had decided against riding out onto the plains to make camp. He figured his enemy would have sentry outposts to prevent his escape, so he spent the rest of the night beside the creek, sleeping with his weapons.

At the first roseate flush of dawn, he tacked the Ovaro and bore west along the creek. Two miles outside of Sublette he rounded a bend and came within a few feet of riding over the McCallister brothers, both sound asleep.

"Up and on the line!" he called out. "Indians on the warpath!"

"Holy Hannah!" Dub cried out, struggling to get out from under his ratty blanket. "Nate, snap into it! We're under attack by redskins!"

"It's still too early, Ma," Nate protested, still half asleep. "That hay field can wait. Le'me sleep longer."

Fargo laughed so hard he almost rolled out of the saddle. "The two bravos from Ohio. If I was an Indian, you'd both be deader than dried herrings."

As he grabbed the horn and swung down, however, Fargo realized the farm boys had picked a good spot. There were scrub oaks and big cottonwoods to screen the horses and plenty of hock-high bunch grass for grazing. The place also offered a clear field of vision in all directions.

Fargo led the Ovaro in among the trees where the two dobbins were grazing. He tethered the stallion and stripped the neck leather, but only loosened the girth. The pad and blanket were still dry, and given the number of enemies at such close quarters, Fargo wanted the saddle in place.

"Mr. Fargo," Dub greeted him, fisting sleep from his eyes, "how'd your, ah, with Rosario go?"

"My, ah, went just fine, junior. You boys made good time."

"We rode all night," Nate chipped in, pulling on his near-worthless boots.

"That's no excuse for letting a man ride right up on your camp. You're in enemy territory now. Did you get your supplies home safe?"

"Yessir. Ma and Krissy was opening an airtight of peaches when we left. Krissy sends her love."

"He don't need it, brother," Dub said. "He's got that pretty faro dealer."

"Keep it up, chucklehead," Fargo warned, "and you'll be wearing your ass for a hat. You boys save any of that grub?"

"Just what we ate on the trail."

"Split these up three ways," Fargo said, handing him the two remaining sandwiches. "They chew like pine pitch and taste like sawdust. But at least it'll put some chuck in our bellies."

When they'd finished eating, Fargo piled up all the weapons and ammo he'd confiscated the night before.

Dub examined one of the Remingtons. "How's come the front sight has been filed off?"

"So it won't snag coming out of the holster," Fargo replied. "Men who fancy themselves quick-draw artists like to do that."

"Pa told us never to bother with the front sight on a handgun— you just point and shoot."

"I agree. Now lissenup, both of you. From now on, always keep a weather eye out for trouble. I killed two jayhawkers last night. At some—"

"How'd you kill the sons of bitches?" Nate cut in eagerly.

"I don't brag on killing. It was just something I had to do, so I did it. Now stick a sock in it and listen. At some point, once they locate us, they're going to rush us. If it was just me, I'd outrun them. My stallion can cross the horizon twice without breaking stride. But those—"

"Aww, c'mon, Mr. Fargo," Nate cut in again, unable to contain himself. "How'd you kill them sage rats? Was it a walking showdown like in *Wild West Tales*?"

"Shut your face, numb nuts," Dub chastised his brother.

"Kiss my ass."

Dub leaped up to attack, but Fargo extended one leg and tripped him. "Save it for the jayhawkers, you damn fools. As I was about to say, those plow nags of yours won't go past a canter. Unless we get you some faster horses, our only chance is to outshoot the bastards. We've got three rifles and five handguns between us with plenty of ammo except for that pinfire I gave you, Nate."

Fargo picked up the Cavalry carbine. "This is an excellent weapon with real stopping power. You load it by thumbing the cartridges through this trap in the butt plate. Holds seven shots. It's got one drawback, though—when it heats up too much, these copper-jacketed slugs tend to stick in the chamber instead of ejecting, and you have to pry the damn things out. So try not to rapid-fire it for too long."

Fargo deftly disassembled the firing-bolt group and showed them how to clean it.

"How long, you think, before they find us?" Dub asked.

"Most of these border ruffian thugs," Fargo replied, "couldn't locate their own asses at high noon in a hall of mirrors. But since there's no place else to hole up, they'll be riding the creek soon enough. I've got a plan to divert them for a while."

Fargo quickly scaled one of the oaks and took a good squint around. So far he'd spotted no sign of trouble.

"This creek takes enough turns to make a cow cross-eyed," he called down to the brothers. "That's good for us. Means we'll have plenty of warning before they're on us."

"Damnation!" Dub said. "We forgot to tell you, Mr. Fargo. We passed three freighters yesterday. They gave us the news about some senator and general, I forget their names."

Fargo hung from a branch and dropped down. "Senator Drummond and General Hoffman, right?"

"Yeah, that's them. You heard too, huh?"

"No. What happened?"

"Well," Dub went on, savoring his importance as a man bearing news, "Cheyenne Indians attacked 'em. Killed 'em all. The senator, the general, and a military guard detail. They was found by a search party from the outpost at Two Buttes."

"Cheyenne Indians," Fargo repeated, his face thoughtful. "How'd they know that?"

"They found a Cheyenne lance."

"A Cheyenne brave," Fargo said, "works for months on his weapons. Any brave who leaves one on the battlefield is the butt of scorn, and Indian braves hate scorn."

"Well, there was arrows, too," Dub continued. "Sticking in the bodies. They all had crow-feather fle—flitch—"

"Fletching," Fargo supplied.

"Yeah, that."

"That ain't all," Nate chimed in. "All the bodies was scalped, and some had their pizzles cut off and shoved into their mouths."

By now Fargo looked skeptical. "Boys, I've been around Plains Indians since I was your age. That attack wasn't by Cheyennes—not likely, anyhow."

"How's come?" Nate asked.

"Scalping is exaggerated in the crapsheets back east. Most tribes don't like it all that much—I've even watched a Sioux warrior puke while trying to do it. They learned it from the Spanish, and it's usually reserved for an especially hated enemy. And right now white men are still mostly a curiosity to the Indian. A Cheyenne would be more likely to demand tribute than to kill—it's a tribe with high regard for human life, even their enemy's."

Fargo paused, trying to fit some pieces into the picture starting to form in his mind. "Still, all Indians are notional, and Cheyennes *could* have scalped them. But the mutilation of the bodies—that's more like Pawnees, Kiowas, or Comanches."

"Then what about the lance and the arrows?" Dub asked.

"Easy to get at any trading post. Were the bodies bullet-shot, too?"

Dub nodded. "Some up to twenty times, the freighters said."

"Then that tears it—it wasn't Cheyennes," Fargo said with finality. "Very few of them have guns yet, and even if they did, they'd never waste ammo like that—it's too hard for an Indian to come by. White men staged that 'Indian' massacre."

"Christ! Why?"

Fargo shook his head. "Where do all lost years go? But I'll bet you a dollar to a doughnut it has something to do with a railroad. Drummond is—was—a big howler for the Kansas-Pacific Railroad. The Rock Island Line out of Illinois is their major competition."

"But are you saying the railroad barons," Dub asked, "would really murder a U.S. senator?"

Fargo shook his head. "They wouldn't do it nor even order it. But their big mistake is in hiring 'agents' to clear the path for them. These agents sometimes act on their own, and the barons don't learn the details."

"I forgot," Dub added. "One soldier musta got away. Them freighters said there was twelve enlisted men, but only eleven bodies."

"That tears it," Fargo declared. "Boys, that bloody pouch in my saddlebag was given to the Quakers by a dying soldier. I still can't prove it, but I'm certain-sure now those jayhawkers pulled the massacres. And the mysterious topkick is a railroad agent who's got the 'butternut guerrillas' on his payroll."

"The filthy sons of bitches," Dub said. "That means whatever's in that pouch could be real important, huh?"

"The way you say. And our murdering band somehow knows I've got it."

"Maybe we'd best try and get it to a fort," Nate suggested.

Fargo shook his head. "I've considered that. But I think we're safer staying around here, playing cat and mouse, than we are making a break for a fort."

"Yeah," Dub agreed. "Me and Nate ain't got the horses for it."

"Which means I'd lose your valuable firepower. And even a fast horse gets tired on the open plains. I'd be like a nit trying to cross a billiards table while the balls are crashing around. And riding hard, with no chance for me to scout terrain ahead, there's a good chance my horse would pull up lame."

"So we just wait?" Nate said.

"Won't be long," Fargo promised him, "and then you'll be sorry the waiting is over."

Fargo was right—the wait wasn't all that long.

Several hours passed, Fargo killing time by pulling out a greasy deck of playing cards and teaching the brothers the rudiments of poker.

"Goddamn but these flats is ugly," Dub declared, gazing all around them. "Ma likes it, though."

"Now that's unusual in a woman," Fargo said. "It's women have the hardest time adjusting to a place without trees and such. I've heard of some to be driven insane by the wide-open spaces."

"Ohio is pretty," Dub said. "They got hills and trees and ponds everywhere. I wish Pa had never pulled up stakes."

Fargo didn't agree that the Great Plains were ugly. Right now, a vast dome of blue sky met the far horizon neat as a lid, and a man could see clear into next week. Each time the wind kicked up, waves moved through the tall grass just like they did on the ocean.

"Ohio is nice country," he agreed, "if you don't mind the way it's peopling up. But you can't judge grasslands by woodlands. Some men like redheads, some men like blondes."

"And a few others," Nate teased, "like 'em all."

Fargo grinned. "Guilty as charged. And I feel the same way about land. Although I admit I wouldn't give you a plugged peso for the Salt Desert out in Mormon country. That place gets so hot a man's ass fries in the saddle. Death Valley is a heller, too. Your deal, Nate."

While Nate shuffled the cards, Fargo again climbed up into the tree for a look around.

"Well, here's the fandango," he called down. "Looks like a patrol of about ten jayhawkers are riding the creek real slow, looking for us."

"Are they close?" Dub asked.

"No, they're about even with the trading post, maybe two miles away. But you know my philosophy."

"Run to the guns," they said in unison.

"*That's* the gait. Nate, hand me up my spyglasses, wouldja? Right saddle pocket."

Taking care to avoid making reflections, Fargo studied the border ruffians. They moved slowly and methodically, searching every inch of the growth. He dwelled on a huge bear of a man whose hair was tied off in a knot behind him.

"The leader of this bunch is definitely Shanghai Webb," Fargo reported to the brothers.

"You know him?" Dub said.

"Just the ugly sight of him. Saw him a few times in San Francisco. He was a leader of the Hounds, the local vigilante bunch. He earned his name there from conking men over the head and selling them to ship captains."

"Think he's the big boss of this bunch?" Nate asked.

"Nah. He led his own gang of scalpers in the border country, and he's a ruthless bastard. But he ain't got the mentality of a mastermind. He's prob'ly the ramrod in the field, but there's a more cunning son of a buck behind the scenes. There's plenty of simoleans, too, and I'd wager it's railroad money."

Fargo traversed the glasses until they focused on a crooked-nosed redhead with a patch over his left eye.

"Here's the roach named Moss," he said. "And the Big Fifty is resting on his pommel. I'd wager he's the jasper that fired on us two days ago, gents. He's trouble—damn near split my melon at eight hundred yards."

Fargo dropped out of the tree.

"We gonna charge 'em?" Dub asked.

"Look, you two," Fargo said, "I guarantee you the time is coming when the three of us will bust caps side by side. But right now I've got a plan that requires just one experienced man—me. You boys just stockpile your guns and ammo and take up good positions just in case."

Fargo crossed to the Ovaro and tugged the Henry out of its boot.

"Just in case what?" Dub demanded.

"In case they kill me," Fargo said matter-of-factly. "If they do, they'll start looking for my horse so's they can find that pouch."

"Won't you be on your horse?"

Fargo shook his head. "Here's the play. I'm gonna advance on foot under the tree cover. They're moving slow. When I'm within range, I'm gonna open fire with all I got. The point is to make 'em think they found my camp. If I know this trash, they'll turn tail and run if one or two are killed. They'll come back in force, but we'll have them lured by a decoy camp. That buys us some time and, with luck, I winnow out a few more jayhawkers."

"What if they do kill you," Nate asked as Fargo quickly checked the loads in his Colt, "and come looking for your horse?"

"I left you two the glasses. Get up in that tree and watch. If I go down, just abandon your plow nags and ride double on my pinto. Stick to cover and bear west along the creek. When you're clear, ride back to your place and rest and feed the stallion. Then one of you take that pouch to Two Buttes."

Nate started to object, but Fargo was already in motion, sprinting through the trees. His long, muscular legs took him forward quickly, and he held his Henry at a high port. Fargo tried to keep a tree or cluster of bushes ahead of him at all times to block their view of him.

He ran for perhaps fifteen minutes, then suddenly heard voices. Fargo slowed to a walk and advanced cautiously, rounding one of the creek's many bends. He could see his enemy through the trees now, cautiously poking into the brush.

Fargo took up a position behind a cottonwood with a lightning-split trunk, laying the barrel of his Henry in the crotch. His finger curled around the trigger as he dropped a bead on a man riding a sorrel. Fargo expelled a long, slow breath and took up the slack. The Henry bucked into his shoulder, and the jayhawker's face was wiped out in a red smear.

Fargo knew the key to this plan was the element of surprise and the rapidity of his fire. He levered, swung the notched sight onto a bearded man and fired again The bullet struck him in the hip and doubled him over his horn.

Shouts of panic and confusion went up, and several horses reared up. Fargo levered, spotted a target, laid his bead—and then his luck ran out when the hammer clicked uselessly on a faulty cartridge.

*Goddamned factory-pressed ammo*, Fargo thought, forced to pry the dud from the breech with his finger since only spent casings went out the ejector port.

He racked the next bullet home and heard another sickening click. Unfortunately, his enemies heard those clicks, too, and suddenly things were happening nineteen to the dozen.

"We found the bastard's camp!" a voice roared out. "His gun's jammed, boys! Rush him!"

Bullets tore chunks out of the tree and sent shards of bark into his eyes. Cursing, but staying frosty, Fargo tossed down the Henry, shucked out his Colt, and expended all six rounds at the wall of men pressing forward. He killed at least one horse and saw another man spin from the saddle, blood pluming from his chest. Two men cried out from wounds.

Not until Fargo expended the last shell in his six-gun did he glimpse the man called Moss in the corner of one eye, sighting in with that lethal Big Fifty at almost point-blank range.

Fargo threw himself to one side at the same moment that Moss fired, the big-bore widow-maker sounding like a cannon at this range. A white-hot wire of pain creased the left side of Fargo's neck, so intense he feared he was killed. But his defiant instinct to fight until the end took over.

Knowing it was his last hope, and praying those faulty shells had no more brothers, Fargo snatched up his Henry, levered, and felt the weapon kick into him. It still held plenty of shells, and with Shanghai Webb's patrol already badly shot up, the jayhawkers wanted no more of this cartridge session.

Even as the wound on his neck dripped blood down his chest, and made Fargo wince in throbbing pain, he heard the hired thugs retreating toward Sublette.

# 8

"Holy Hannah, Mr. Fargo!" Nate exclaimed. "We thought you was a gone beaver when them sons of Satan charged the trees. So many guns was poppin' it sounded like river ice breaking apart."

"Didn't I tell you lead tends to fly around me?"

"Some of it didn't quite make it around you," Dub said, staring at his neck.

Nate said, "Wasn't you scared?"

"Chappies, when my Henry quit on me I damn near pissed myself," Fargo admitted. "And when Moss hit me in the neck with that big slug, I figured my toes would soon be pointed to the sky. Turns out he only grazed me."

"It's big and long," Dub reported, making a closer study of the wound. "But it ain't deep. Not much blood, neither."

"Good. That means it won't mortify. Nate, run down to the creek, wouldja, and pry some moss off those rocks."

Fargo packed the wound with moss and tied it in place with one of the linen bandage strips he carried in his possibles bag.

"This is the second time today I've had 'moss' on my neck," he quipped. "You know what they say: a hair off the dog."

Nate looked puzzled. "When did you put moss on your neck earlier?"

Fargo shook his head. "A mind like a steel trap."

"Think them jayhawkers will come back today?" Dub asked.

Fargo mulled that. "I penetrated one of the puke gangs once in Missouri," he replied. "I had to spring a female captive. One thing I noticed, the leadership's authority hangs by a thread."

"I don't take your meaning."

"There's no loyalty, no duty involved. It's just a criminal clan of back-shooting, coyote-bitten skunks. That means they sull when the going gets rough—they have to be bribed with money and liquor. I killed at least two men today, and wounded three more—some of them serious, and out here that spells death. So at least four are killed in the last two days alone, maybe more."

"Now I take your drift. These peckerwoods will prob'ly liquor up today and tonight. Pa called that Dutch courage."

Fargo nodded. "Which makes me wonder . . . by tonight their whiskey jollification should be well along, so maybe us three should make it a little jollier?"

Nate's eyes grew as large as pesos. "You mean attack them?"

"Well, call it a serenade if that sounds better."

"I think it's smart thinking," Dub put in. "Mr. Fargo rattled their gourds good today. Why not take it to them while they're still jumpy."

Fargo nodded. "Now you're whistling."

The Trailsman said nothing to worry the brothers, but just as Indians did he hated this "forting up" business. He had spent most of his time out beyond the known settlements, always needful of pushing over the next ridge, always ducking the ultimate arrow, seldom sleeping under a roof. Holing up like this and waiting was slow torture—and often a recipe for defeat.

"But do you have any idea where they're holed up?" Dub asked.

"I might at that."

It was Fargo's way to make a mental map of any area he rode through, and he had crossed these plains numerous times.

"I can't be sure," he admitted. "But about ten miles or so due east of here there's a big motte of pines. In the middle of the pines there's an old dugout from last century, winter headquarters for traders. It's a perfect place to hole up."

"We hit tonight?" Nate asked.

"Hold your powder, boy. Maybe, maybe not. When you're stepping into a river, you never put your foot down until you're sure there's a rock to hold it. Before we serenade these jayhawkers, I'm going to scout ahead."

Brassy afternoon sunlight coaxed out the furnace heat of the hard-baked September plains. Fargo closed his sleepy eyes for a moment and listened to the orchestra of the flat land: the lulling crackle of insects, the bubbling chuckle of the creek, the soft song of the prairie wind. It seemed unreal to him that, only a short time ago, he had been in a life-or-death shooting scrape here. Some said the West was foreign to men, but in truth, men were foreign to the West.

"Mr. Fargo?"

Reluctantly, Fargo forced his eyes open. "Yeah, Nate?"

"The first day we rode in—you said there was draw-shoot killers in that saloon where we ate."

"Yeah. What of it?"

"There's some in the border ruffians, too, ain't there?"

"Some. But drawing fast isn't the main mile. It's how fast you get off a shot that counts. And you boys've got the edge there."

"I'm not worried about no draw-shoot killers," Dub boasted. "But I am sorta perplexed about our horses. They ain't—"

"No need to get your pennies in a bunch," Fargo assured him. "Whatever plan we come up with will cover our escape. First, though, I have to scout and get the lay of the land. This thing can't be done slapdash."

With the exception of a few isolated riders, all of whom swung wide of the creek, there was no more activity on the plains surrounding Sublette for the rest of that day.

After dark, Fargo built a small fire in a pit and made corn dodgers and coffee.

"You was right, Mr. Fargo," Dub said while the three men ate. "They didn't try to flush us again. Prob'ly workin' up that Dutch courage Pa told us about."

"When you riding out?" Nate asked.

"When I'm ready."

"Can't we go, too? We ain't never done no scouting."

Fargo grunted. "Which is exactly why you're not going. It's no job for pilgrims. Your ma will skin me alive if I get you killed."

"Damn it all to hell anyhow!" Nate exploded. "Hell, all we're doing is washing bricks."

"Good. I like clean bricks."

"Yeah, but you said—"

"What did you expect when you asked to side me, a sugar

tit? Nate, this ain't frontier school I'm running here. We're at war, and war out here is one of two things: scary as hell or boring as hell. Mostly it's boring."

"Yeah, I noticed."

"Shut up, knucklehead," Dub snapped at his younger brother. "We'll get our turn when Mr. Fargo comes back."

"That's the straight," Fargo said. "Nate, your hour will come. Believe me, scouting is not all beer and skittles. It takes years to get good at it. Besides, with more than one man, there's too big a chance of getting caught."

Fargo drank a second, a third cup of strong black coffee to keep him alert. Then he wrapped his head to improve his night vision. When a nascent moon, white as new snow, appeared low in the indigo sky, Fargo scooped up mud from the creek bank and smeared his faced with it to cut reflection.

The Ovaro was already saddled, and Fargo had only to tighten the girth. He slipped the bridle on, and the stallion took the bit easily, eager to work out the kinks. Fargo stepped up into leather.

"I'm off like a dirty shirt. Keep your weapons close to hand, boys," he told the brothers. "It's not likely they'll make a play after dark, but be ready. I should be back in a couple of hours. If I don't show by an hour before sunup, you'll know I'm dead. Light a shuck out of here while it's still dark, or they'll shoot you to streamers."

"And just *leave* you here," Dub protested.

"Yeah, that's an order. 'I' won't be here by then—just a slab of cold meat leaving a lot of disappointed women."

"Can we have Rosario?" Dub asked hopefully.

Fargo grinned as he gigged the Ovaro across the creek. "Young man, she'd eat you alive."

Fargo bore east across the moonlit plains, letting the Ovaro run for a few minutes, then reining him back to a trot to conserve his wind if it was needed. The Trailsman's vigilant eyes left nothing alone, and several times he was able to avoid sudden sand wallows: places where the grass had died and formed pockets of loose sand that could trip up a horse.

Fargo could make out the pine motte well before he reached it: a dark, shadowy mass against the slightly lighter plains. As he drew near, he could make out fires—perhaps seven or eight— back within the trees. There could be sentries on the outer edge, but Fargo took that chance and moved within a hundred yards or so.

He reined in and dismounted, hobbling the Ovaro foreleg to rear. Then, to cover some of the Ovaro's larger splashes of white, he unrolled his blanket and tossed it over the stallion.

"Sorry about that tight girth, old campaigner," he said softly, patting the pinto's neck. "But we might have to make a hot bust out."

The stalwart Ovaro merely nuzzled his shoulder, inured to such necessities.

Fargo reluctantly left his Henry behind, knowing from long experience it would impede swift, easy movement. As he drew near the mass of trees, he could hear the familiar sounds of drunken revelry: shouts, laughter, catcalls, men singing bawdy choruses of "Lu-lu Girl" and "She Had Freckles on Her Butt I Love Her."

Fargo reached the pine trees and hid behind one of them, deciding on the best course of movement and concealment. The motte was actually five concentric circles of trees with about thirty feet of clearing between each ring. Except for an apparent sentry on his right, so drunk he was practically walking on his knees, all of the jayhawkers were seated around campfires within the first three rings.

And at the hub, Fargo guessed, was the dugout where the king rat and his favorite rodents stayed.

He knew he had to work his way in closer for a better reconnoiter. Leapfrogging from tree to tree he penetrated into the third ring. Clay and corncob pipes were lit everywhere, and Fargo whiffed cheap, foul-smelling Mexican tobacco.

"Never mind Fargo's reputation," growled a voice like rough gravel at a fire just left of him. "A fish always looks bigger underwater."

"We'll fix his wagon, all right," replied a slurring drunk. "And with him planted, them other two are ducks on a fence. I plan to cut off Fargo's nuts and use the cured sac for a coin purse."

A third man chimed in. "I'm gonna carve out his teeth for a necklace. Then I say we bury him up to his neck in an anthill and soak his head in honey."

"Yeah, but you got to admit," called out a voice from a neighboring fire, "Fargo's got sand."

"Listen to this sissy-bitch! A Sioux papoose has a bigger set on him. Fargo just got lucky today, that's all. Even a blind hog will root up an acorn now and then."

Fargo couldn't help an ironic grin as he moved deeper into the trees, recording every detail of the layout in his mind's eye. If he was captured tonight, he realized, half of his body parts would end up as souvenirs.

To preserve his night vision as much as possible, Fargo tried to avoid looking into the fires. Nonetheless, he scooted up to the next tree and literally bumped into a man taking a leak.

Fargo's face went cold, and he raised his right foot, getting a grip on the haft of his Arkansas toothpick. He'd have to cut this thug's throat wide open before he could give the shout.

"Watch it, you clumsy son of a bitch," the jayhawker muttered, not even bothering to look at him. "Go drain your snake somewheres else—this is my tree."

"Sorry." Fargo scooted ahead, pressing toward the still-hidden dugout. In this heat the entrance was likely open. If not, there had to be some kind of ventilation hole. He wanted to see the face behind the Quaker massacre—and the slaughter of Senator Drummond and General Hoffman and God knew how many others.

Fargo crept on cat feet into the inner ring and spotted the exposed portion of the sturdy log dugout.

Just then, however, his attention was arrested by the sound of sobbing—female sobbing.

"Well, God kiss me," he muttered.

Guided by his hearing, Fargo shifted to his left and saw her in the moonlight: a slender young blonde in a torn and filthy white dress, her wrists tied with ropes to a tree behind her.

"Don't scream, lady," Fargo said as he moved in. "I'm a friend."

A pretty but dirty, tear-streaked face turned toward him. "Oh, please," she begged. "Don't do it! Just kill me."

"Damn it, keep your voice down," Fargo admonished. "I said I'm a friend. I'm not with this bunch."

His point sank in, and tears of relief cascaded down her cheeks.

"Oh, sir, these monsters murdered my husband right in front of me. They're all filthy, depraved monsters, but their leader is . . . he's not even . . ."

"Shush it," Fargo said gently but firmly. "This is no time to be talking. We're both far from safe."

Even as he cut the ropes with his knife, however, Fargo felt the weight of an excruciating choice. To this point he had been feeling triumphant. These border ruffians were so drunk they were useless, and their tight groups around the fires made them easy targets. By placing crack shots like Dub and Nate in the right spots, the three of them could mount more than the harassing raid Fargo originally envisioned: they could have killed and wounded virtually every man here. And under territorial law, Fargo could then have arrested or killed the leaders in that dugout.

Now, however, one innocent life had changed all that.

Fargo knew the grim reality. This girl was weak and helpless, and there was no sanctuary for her in these parts. The only choice, if he decided to save her, was the McCallister place, some thirty miles distant. Yet, the Code of the West, the code Fargo lived by and had helped to define, was clear: at any and all costs, women and children must be saved from harm. A man who violated that code was no man at all—he became like the hell-spawned scum surrounding Fargo now.

"Can you walk?" he asked her.

"I've been tied in one position for days. But I'll try."

It was no use—she couldn't even get to her feet without collapsing.

"Stay quiet," Fargo warned, picking her up and tossing her over his left shoulder to free his gun hand. The fragile young woman was light as a handful of feathers.

Fargo swept wide of the campfires and was soon out on the open plains.

"What's your name, miss?" he asked as he jogged toward the Ovaro.

"Cynthia Henning. Cindy."

"I'm Skye Fargo."

"Oh, God sent you, Mr. Fargo. I know He did! I prayed and I prayed that a decent man would come help me."

Fargo considered himself a pagan, but he was open to the possibility of a Creator. And if God did send him on a divine mission, that made it easier to accept the fact that he just *might* have destroyed this gang tonight.

"We're out of the woods as a matter of fact," he said, "but

we're not out of the woods as a manner of speaking—not just yet. Can you stand a long ride tonight, behind me in the saddle?"

"I'll try, Mr. Fargo, with all my might. But I'm weak—they gave me food, but I couldn't eat it. I've had no food or sleep in four days. But, by all things holy, I'll try."

"Good girl."

Fargo reached the Ovaro and set her on the ground while he quickly rolled his blanket back up and fastened it with the cantle straps. Then he gave the girl water before he lifted her into the saddle. "Grab tight to the horn, Cindy, until I get aboard with you."

He untied the hobbles, turned the stirrup, and stepped into it, carefully easing himself into the saddle in front of her.

"Put both arms around me and lean forward," Fargo told her. "And keep talking to me so I'll know how you're doing. If you pass out, you could fall from the saddle and get hurt."

Hoping those two-legged swine wouldn't miss their pretty captive too soon, Fargo reined the Ovaro around and headed back to see the McCallister boys.

Now that the girl felt safe, at least for the time being, her fear eased and exhaustion tried to claim her. Several times, despite his efforts to keep her talking, Fargo had to bunch the reins in one hand so he could grab her when she slumped.

"Cindy!" he snapped at one point, cuffing her gently with one hand. "Those owlhoots could realize you're gone at any minute. We've got to get clear of here in a puffin' hurry. Stay awake."

"I'm sorry, Skye. I'm just so . . . tired."

"I know, hon, but stay awake. You should be safe in a few hours."

"Safe," she repeated as if it were the finest word in all the world.

Fargo knew, however, that not every jayhawker was wallowing back in the pine woods, drunk as the Lords of Creation. A few were surely on roving sentry, patrolling the escape routes around Sublette. He might even encounter one now, on his way back to the camp by the creek, and with a half-conscious girl to hold in the saddle he couldn't count on the Ovaro's breakneck speed or his own ability to use his weapons.

Eyes constantly scanning for the skyline of riders, Fargo held the Ovaro to a fast trot—there was a long ride ahead to the McCallister place. And although Cindy was a mere slip of a girl (*woman*, Fargo corrected himself, feeling her pleasing feminine form pressing into his back), it was still extra weight his stallion wasn't accustomed to.

Fargo tried to keep her talking, avoiding any questions about whatever happened to her and sticking to inconsequential matters. Now and then she rallied, tightening her grip on him and responding to his questions.

"Hallo, McCallister boys!" he shouted when he neared the camp. "It's Fargo—hold your powder!"

They splashed through the sparkling creek and up into the trees. Dub and Nate each had a gun to hand.

"Any trouble here?" Fargo asked, dismounting and reaching up to grab Cindy and stretch her out in the grass.

"A sentry rode by once," Dub replied, staring at the girl. "Who's she?"

"Her name's Cindy Henning. She was a captive at the jay-hawkers' headquarters."

"How can she stay here with us?"

"She can't, chucklehead. I'm taking her to your place. Tonight—right now. I aim to be back before sunrise."

"Damnation!" Nate exclaimed. "You said that tonight me and Dub could—"

"Cinch your lips, Nate. That was before I knew about her."

"Shit! We ain't never gonna see no action."

"Take a good look at her," Fargo ordered. "Both of you."

"She's pretty," Dub conceded.

"That's not my point. See that black eye? See how dirty and nerve-frazzled she looks?"

Both boys nodded, the resentment easing from their faces.

Fargo said, "I'd wager she's about Dub's age, but look how those heartless bastards have aged her in just a few days. They murdered her husband right in front of her."

"Jesus Criminy," Nate said. "Did they . . . ?"

"I don't know and I don't give a damn. Boys, if you're going to be decent Western men, you have to understand that a woman in trouble—any woman, never mind her looks or station in life—is your responsibility when she's in a tight fix. If this was your sister, your daughter, your wife—would you want able-bodied men to abandon her to her fate just so they could see the elephant?"

Nate looked ashamed. "Of course not. Men ain't s'pose to do that to women. I'd kill any man that done Ma or Krissy that way."

"Damn straight," Dub chimed in.

"Now you're talking sense."

In truth, however, Fargo's little spiel was directed at himself as much as to the McCallister brothers. His sense of regret was sharp—this gang could have been destroyed tonight, but now the fight would drag on. Nor could he forget his utter helplessness, three days ago, as he watched innocent Quaker girls being brutally raped. He was bound and determined to get this girl safely out of here.

"All right, boys," Fargo said, forking leather, "hand her up to me."

With Cindy in the saddle behind him, Fargo met first Dub's, then Nate's eyes. They were fresh off the turnip wagon, and he hated leaving them here alone. But both young men had courage, and he knew they were dead aims.

"You're on your own until morning, boys. Cover your ampersands."

Dub's jaw firmed in the moonlight. "Them bastards mess with the McCallister boys, we'll shoot 'em to couch stuffin's."

"Good luck, Mr. Fargo," Nate added. "Tell Ma and Krissy 'hey.' They'll nurse that girl back to health. They're dyin' for company."

Fargo headed west into the black velvet folds of darkness, knowing trouble lay out there somewhere and hoping he could steer wide of it.

# 9

Fargo stuck close to the creek at first, taking advantage of the cover. He took his bearings from the dog star and the pole star, two fixed reference points he would need when he had to turn north from the creek.

The night wind had cooled and picked up in force, reviving Cindy somewhat. "Skye?"

"Hmm?"

"I heard you talking to those boys back there. What you said about protecting women—it was wonderful."

Embarrassed, Fargo tried to laugh it off. "Now, see, I only said all that because I knew you were listening."

"Fibber."

"All the time," he confessed.

She lapsed into a long silence, and Fargo feared she was blacking out.

"It's best for you to keep talking," he reminded her.

"All right, I heard something else, too. One of the boys wondered if I had been, you know . . . ravished. I still can't believe it, being's how I was a prisoner for several days, but I never was. It was coming close, though, and I have you to thank for getting out in time."

"For your sake I'm mighty glad to hear that," Fargo assured her. "But what made them wait?"

"My black eye."

Fargo looked back at her, puzzled. "Maybe you could spell that out a little plainer?"

"Well, the man who's in charge of those monsters—"

"Cindy, pardon me all to hell for interrupting you, but I've been waiting for you to bring him up on your own. I have to ask while you're still awake—do you know his name?"

71

"The men who . . . who killed my husband and abducted me called him Belloch. I assume that's his last name."

The fingers of Fargo's memory flipped through all the file cards and found nothing. "Means nothing to me. What's he look like?"

"He's a natty dresser and well groomed, but something about him made me think of the serpent in the Garden of Eden. He's tall and very thin, about your age, with a spade beard, I think it's called. Eyes as dead as buttons. There's a dagger sticking from one of his boots, but I noticed no other weapons. And that brothel stink of his lilac hair tonic—I'll smell that forever."

"All right, I'll remember all that about him. Now back to that black eye and how it saved you."

He felt her pointy breasts press into his back as she fortified herself with a deep breath. "The first night of my captivity, he came out to . . . to inspect me. He unbuttoned my dress and used that dagger to cut away my chemise and petticoat. He then . . . ran his hands all over me and felt my—my bosom for a long time. I was sure he meant to . . . you know."

"We both know," Fargo said. "Why didn't he? Frankly, I can't believe you didn't measure up to his standards."

"Skye, he said my black eye had to fade first. He said, 'I don't poke bruised fruit.' "

"Jesus." Fargo felt his scalp tighten at the perversity of it. "This Belloch must only have one oar in the water."

"Yes, thankfully. And after he buttoned my dress back up, he whispered in my ear, 'Life is a disease, and the only cure is death.' "

"*No* oars in the water," Fargo amended. "I don't mind going up against a run-of-the-mill murderer, but these sick-brain types give me the fantods. You can't predict them."

"Well anyway, you came in the nick of time, Skye. He said one more day and my bruise would fade. After he sated his filthy lust, one of his lackeys was to kill me after he, too, 'had a whack at me,' as Belloch put it."

"Don't worry," Fargo assured her. "He'll get his comeuppance real soon now."

But secretly her words troubled Fargo. He meant what he had told her: He had dealt with all manner of enemies on the wild frontier, and none were more formidable than the criminally insane.

The Ovaro was keeping a good canter now, still holding up well and showing no signs of lathering. But the creek had taken a sharp jog to the south, leaving them on the open plains. With no reference points on the ground, they could have ridden in circles all night. But Fargo was adept at star navigating and kept them on course, due west, toward the Cimarron.

The problem was, they still weren't all that far outside of Sublette—and clear of any roving sentries. Fargo felt a cold fist grip his heart when a voice boomed out, "Halt!"

Cindy's embrace on him tightened with fear. But since Fargo couldn't see their enemy, he relied on the near-total darkness as he thumped the Ovaro's ribs, opening him out to a dead run.

A six-gun spoke its piece, and when the bullet snapped just overhead, he realized his mistake: Cindy's dress, though filthy, still showed plenty of white.

"Halt, you son of a bitch!" the voice roared.

"Lean forward with me, Cindy!" Fargo called out, bending down over the horn. He was in no position to go toe-to-toe with his attacker.

A third shot rang out, the bullet kicking the stirrup out from under Fargo's left foot. He could hear the rataplan of hooves behind them. This time, however, Fargo spotted a streak of muzzle flash, and now he had a target area.

He jerked back his short gun. But Fargo had a life depending on him, and he took no chances. In these inky fathoms of darkness, a horse was a much more likely target, and that's what he aimed for, snapping off three quick rounds.

The hoofbeats behind them suddenly grew erratic, turned into skidding noises, then stopped completely.

"I stopped him," Fargo said. "Lucky shot, but it worked."

But the sentry was still alive, so Fargo hadn't stopped the danger. Only a heart skip after Fargo's remark, a shrill blast from a tin horn disrupted the silence of the plains.

The Ovaro shuddered at the ear-piercing sound.

"Is he signaling to the men in the woods?" Cindy asked, fear spiking her voice up an octave.

"Nah, they're too far away. He's calling all the roving sentries into this area."

"What will we do?"

"The only thing we can do—outrun them until we lose them."

"If we don't," Cindy said close to his ear, for it was hard to hear above the Ovaro's galloping hooves, "Skye, I'm begging you—kill me before you let those filthy murderers capture me again."

Fargo had trusted his life to the Ovaro in many daunting circumstances, and this night he did so again. But it was a dangerous roll of the dice. He had heard at least two pursuers behind them, and more lead had whiffed past them, but his redoubtable steed eventually exhausted the pursuers' horses. Unfortunately, in eluding them Fargo had to veer off course from the path he and the McCallister boys had followed in their ride to Sublette.

Farther west than he wanted to be, the Cimarron behind them, Fargo was riding in near-total darkness. For starters, he loathed riding in unscouted country even in daylight. Despite the lack of trees, they cropped up now and then, and a few years back Fargo and the Ovaro had once ridden smack into one, both sustaining injuries. And a low-hanging branch could sweep him and Cindy right out of the saddle, or knock Fargo senseless.

The real danger, however, was the ground. A horse's most vulnerable piece of anatomy was its thin legs. A jagged stone in the wrong place could make the Ovaro pull up lame; a prairie dog hole could snap a leg completely and force Fargo to shoot him. There was also danger from sudden sand wallows. The Trailsman held his now tiring stallion to a trot and struggled to read the darkness all around them.

Cindy was near "foundering," too. Horsebacking at a hard pace was hard even for a man used to it. The fragile girl, however, had probably moved about only in conveyances before this. The fast clip and jarring motion, in her exhausted condition, had induced a delirious half sleep.

"Tom?" she called out. "Tom, will you take me to the cider party next week at the Hupenbecker barn?"

"With pleasure," Fargo replied, figuring Tom must be the young widow's newly murdered husband.

"Then here's a big hug for you."

Fargo felt a sudden surge of blood into his manhood and had to shift in the saddle when she pressed herself hard against him. He wished he had met this delicate beauty under happier circumstances—Belloch had cut away all of her underclothing, and it was easy to feel every swelling and curve under that thin dress. Especially with her right hand bumping against the tent in his buckskins . . .

*Put it out of your mind, Fargo,* he told himself. *The way she's feeling right now, she just might do it with you. Then, after, she'll think of her husband, who never even got a grave, and hate herself.*

"Tom?" she mumbled. "Since we're engaged to be married, why shouldn't we see each other naked? I've never seen a grown man's . . . you know. Ma says they get real big when a man's excited. Tom?"

"We best not, Cindy," Fargo said reluctantly, cursing his confounded luck. "We might go too far."

"Then let's go too far! Even if I catch a baby, we're getting married in a month."

"Cindy," Fargo said, "let's talk about that cider party again, all right?"

Fortunately for a randy-in-the-saddle Fargo, she began rambling about her wedding dress. For the past hour heat lightning had been shimmering on the horizon. The air still felt soft as the breath of a young girl, but Fargo knew that hazy ring around the moon meant hard wind and rain before morning.

He had hoped to outrun it, but all at once a huge clap of thunder rocked the plains, startling Cindy awake.

"Dig my slicker out from behind you," he told her, raising his voice above the sound of the sudden wind. "Wrap yourself up in it and get set for a hell-buster."

She had just finished protecting herself in his oilskin poncho when the first sheets of rain began slanting down. Soon, sudden wind gusts drove the rain almost horizontally, stinging Fargo's face like buckshot. He pulled the brim of his hat down and tucked his face toward his left shoulder.

"Skye," she shouted behind him, "can you even see?"

"No," he admitted. "But I wasn't seeing much before this, either. We'll have to trust my stallion now. Just be glad a horse's eyes are on the sides of his head."

"Shouldn't we stop until it lets up? You're getting soaked."

"Nah. These are big raindrops, and that usually means a quick rain. There's no shelter, anyway. Besides, I don't want those two boys alone after sunup."

"I caused all this trouble. I'm sorry."

"Not you," Fargo corrected her. "The pond scum who abducted you caused all this. I'm honored to help you."

"You're a wonderful man, Skye Fargo."

"You've noticed that?" Fargo joked, eliciting a weak laugh from the exhausted girl.

But she might not think he was so wonderful, Fargo thought, if the azimuth he was following was inaccurate. Until the storm blew over, he couldn't even check the stars. Everything now was guesswork, and finding one small farm, on the Great Plains, was like looking for a sliver in an elephant's ass.

Hard storms that came quickly often stopped quickly, and this one blew over in thirty minutes. Fargo swiped water from his eyes and spotted a slightly darker mass against the night sky—a mass about the size of the McCallister barn.

"Something's up ahead," Fargo told Cindy. "Cross your fingers."

By now the Ovaro was so tired that Fargo could feel flecks of lather blowing back on him. But the game stallion kept up the strut. There was a sudden eruption of barking, and Fargo grinned—Dan'l Boone was at his post.

"Hallo, McCallisters!" he called out. "It's Skye Fargo riding in."

As the Ovaro trotted into the bare-dirt yard, Lorena McCallister emerged from the barn with a lantern in one hand, her long Jennings rifle in the other. Krissy followed wearing a long nightshirt, her hair a wild black profusion.

"Trouble, Skye?" Lorena asked, watching Fargo help a pretty, sore-used blonde from the saddle.

"Plenty for this young lady, Lorena. Her name is Cindy Henning. Border ruffians killed her husband and abducted her. Any chance she can stay here for a while until she recovers her strength?"

"Any chance? We'd be pleased to have her stay as long as she cares to, poor thing."

The "poor thing" in question had held up for this hard ride, but now she had reached the limits of endurance. As Fargo was tugging the slicker off Cindy, her knees abruptly buckled and she passed out. He caught her in the nick of time.

"Bring her inside," Lorena said, hurrying on ahead. "Plenty of empty beds."

Krissy followed Fargo in, flashing him that come-hither smile that he remembered well from his first visit.

"She's mighty pretty," Krissy whispered. "Or hadn't you noticed?"

"No shortage of pretty ladies around here, either," Fargo whispered back. "Not to mention shapely."

"But around here it's just going to waste, don't you agree?"

"No misdoubting that," Fargo agreed.

Lorena led him to the living quarters at the end of the barn. "Put her on Dub's bed, right there. It's only a corn-husk mattress, but I doubt she'll mind that for right now, poor thing."

"Right now she could sleep on a rock pile," Fargo said. "Says she hasn't slept in days."

"She'll come sassy with some rest and hot broth. Then we'll feed her up on some of those provisions you sent back. Skye, are the boys all right?"

"They're fine, but I won't lie to you, Lorena—all three of us are up against it near Sublette. Or soon will be."

"Jayhawkers?"

He nodded.

Lorena and Krissy exchanged a troubled glance. Word about them, and the pukes of Missouri, had reached all of the far-flung settlers.

"Well," Lorena finally said, "I'm scared for 'em—they're so young. But their pa was fighting Indians at their age. Boys have to grow into men fast in these parts."

Fargo agreed. No star men, few soldiers, no hemp committees, even—who else was going to stop this butchering trash? As Cindy and those Quakers proved, somebody had to, or the entire West would become one giant criminal empire.

"Have they been a thorn in your side?" Lorena asked.

"Nothing you wouldn't expect from two frisky colts. They're good lads. As soon as I feed and rest my horse, I'm returning to them."

Lorena clucked her tongue. "Skye Fargo, you look almost as worn out as this girl! The creek out back is permanently dry, but there's a seep spring nearby we use for bathing. Krissy, get some soap and a towel and show Skye where it is."

"But my horse—"

"Never you mind. I'll take good care of him. We've got some

oats, and after I dry him off and rub him down, I'll take a curry-comb to him and get those witch's bridles out of his coat. When you finish, Skye, I'll give you a hot meal."

Krissy took Fargo's hand and gave it a promissory squeeze. "Come along, Skye."

They went out the south door of the barn, Fargo studying Krissy in the moonlight. She wasn't as delicate as Cindy, but like the blonde she was right out of the top drawer.

"Must have been rough, huh?" she said.

"What?"

"Having that pretty, nearly naked girl pressed up against you the whole way from Sublette."

"Oh, I was a trouper and endured it."

"I wish it could have been me. When a girl rides straddle, you know, it gets her, well . . . all het up. All that up-and-down rubbing."

Fargo slanted a glance at her. "You are a little firecracker, are'n'cha?"

"I have a very short fuse, if that's what you mean."

"In case you notice me walking funny," Fargo informed her, "it's all your fault."

"Oh?" she said with exaggerated innocence.

"And why bother with a horse?" he added. "Won't a man do?"

She tossed back her pretty head and laughed. The moonlight was brighter now, after the storm, and Fargo saw even little teeth white as pearls. "Men are just fine if a gal can find any. Here's the bathing pool, Skye."

The pool alongside the creek glimmered in the moonlight.

"Well," Fargo said reluctantly, "I guess you'll be heading back? Lorena might not take kindly to—"

Krissy laughed again. "Don't be foolish, Skye. Ma's as man-starved as I am. She didn't send me back to hold the soap."

"I've done my duty," Fargo surrendered.

"Wet buckskins must be hard to take off," she said. "Let Krissy help."

She dropped to her knees and untied his fly. With a sharp tug she pulled his trousers down, revealing his aroused manhood.

"Oh . . . my . . . !" she exclaimed. "Are most men this big?"

"Believe me, darlin', I'm not in the habit of checking."

"It's leaping up and down!" She put one hand around his shaft. "And hard as a horseshoe! My talk did get you all steamed up, didn't it?"

Her hand squeezed him tighter, shooting rays of hot pleasure back into Fargo's groin. Then her head bobbed forward as she took the tip into her hot, moist mouth. Her teeth nipped him gently while she kept stroking. Now the welling pleasure was so overwhelming that Fargo's calves felt like water, and it was hard to remain standing.

By now Krissy was panting. She grabbed Fargo's hands. "You're tired, Skye. Lie down on your back in the grass and let me do all the work."

"I like a take-charge woman," he said agreeably, doing as told.

Krissy grabbed the nightshirt and pulled it over her head. Fargo marveled at her full, heavy tits, the deep-curving hips, the dark triangle at the top of her thighs. She dropped to her knees and cocked one leg to straddle him.

"My lands, Skye, I can barely get high enough to clear you!"

However, she managed, rubbing his tip with the outer folds of her ready sex before bending him to just the right angle and easing down on him.

"Oh, that's nice!" she cried, shoving even more of him into her. "It feels like you're past my belly button."

Pleasure jolted through Fargo's shaft and groin as the walls of her sex, feeling like a tight velvet glove, began a squeeze-and-release that soon had Fargo groaning and Krissy gasping with pleasure as she popped off climaxes in rapid succession. She bent forward far enough to hang her succulent globes in Fargo's face. He took a pliant nipple into his mouth.

"Bite it?" she begged. "Not hard—just little—oh, yes, Skye, just like *that*!"

Unable to contain her passion any longer, she pistoned up and down hard and fast, impaling him from the base of his shaft to the very tip. Fargo felt that tight tingling in his groin that meant release was imminent. When the explosion came he almost bucked her off him.

"Well, Skye Fargo," she said when she could finally speak. "I hope a woman wantin' to be on top don't offend you?"

"No, indeed, pretty lady. I wish more women liked to do it."

"How long you plan on resting your horse?"

"A couple hours. He needs more, but that's all I can spare."

"Best take your bath, then. Here, pull your shirt and boots off and slide into the water, I'll scrub you off. Maybe you'll get hard again, and I'll take care of it for you. Then you can come up and eat before you nap a little."

Fargo grinned as she began sudsing his back, his manhood already stirring like a snake coming awake. "Oh, thanks to you, Miss McCallister, I'll sleep like a baby."

# 10

It was still well before dawn when Rafe Belloch, face choleric with rage, roused his "lieutenants" and ordered them to his dugout.

"Explain this one to me," he demanded. "I woke up early and decided to visit with my female captive. But when I went around back, all I found were cut ropes. Any theories on that?"

An awkward silence followed his question. None of his minions knew where to aim his gaze, so they all stared at the dirt floor.

"She must be gone," Jake suggested in his hillman's twang, fingering the leathery human ears dangling from his belt.

Belloch halted his pacing, staring at Jake with eyes like two pools of burning acid. "Ketchum, your rapier wit is matched only by your superior breeding."

All three men, in their own way, had learned that Belloch liked to engage in "private irony"—it wasn't always clear when a fellow was supposed to laugh, and none of them laughed now.

"Boss, if you're thinking we took her," Shanghai Webb said, "or any of the men—"

"That's not what I'm thinking. In fact, I know exactly who took her."

"Fargo?"

"Who the hell else?" Belloch fumed. "Do you know of any other crusaders around here, or perhaps wood nymphs spirited her away?"

Jake opened his mouth to ask a question, but Shanghai poked an elbow into his side.

Belloch began pacing rapidly, hands clasped behind his back. "Use those goddamn useless melons you call heads and think about it. Fargo could not have known about the woman, could he? Which means what?"

All three men, sleepy and hungover, stood there in stupid silence, not understanding Belloch's point.

"It means, you goddamn toadstools, he was probably on his way to kill me. But, being a 'noble' bastard, he had to save the woman."

"Then we should keep one tied up back there all the time," Jake interjected. "I hear Fargo can't say no to a juicy bit of quim."

Belloch halted and stared at his subordinate. "Jake, you're testing the limits of my patience. You, of all people, shouldn't treat this as a joking matter. If I'm killed, you three go back to the old life. How many gold shiners were in your pockets?"

"Don't make sense nohow," Moss Harper said. "That means he sneaked past our sentries and through the whole camp."

"He did a hell of a lot more than that. While you drunken sots were building your golden calf last night, Fargo got past the outer ring of sentries and escaped the entire area."

"Golden calf?" Jake repeated, his face confused. "What—"

"Shut pan," Shanghai snapped at him. He looked at Rafe. "Christ sakes, boss, you think he's delivering that pouch?"

Rafe heaved a frustrated sigh. "I'm making a gamble that he isn't. I'd say he's coming back here after taking the girl to safety somewhere."

"Prob'ly topping her right now," Jake said. "We'll teach that bastard he better check the brand before he drives another man's stock. He—"

"Jake, you muttonhead," Belloch cut him off, "forget about the woman. She's not the main issue."

"Boss, Fargo is shiftier than a creased buck," Shanghai said. "Why you think he's coming back here?"

"According to Jubilee Lofley, the sentry who tried to stop him, there was only one horse. But Fargo has a couple of farm boys with him. I don't think he'd leave them here very long— his type is loyal to his trail companions."

"That rings right," Shanghai said. "He's hell-bent on settling the Quaker account, and if he's looked in that pouch, he'll have fresh ammo for his crusading."

Belloch nodded. "Yes, and he's the type who likes to paddle

his own canoe rather than call in authorities. His little raid last night proves that."

"Don't make sense," Moss repeated. "Fires was burning everywhere, and guards was posted."

"It makes perfect sense. All of you were Indian drunk last night. Moss, I saw you take a crap in another man's hat. That's a feat to be proud of."

"No need to get on your high horse. You told us to cut the wolf loose last night, so that's what we done."

"Keep a civil tongue in your head," Belloch snapped. "I said cut it loose, not join the pack."

He paced in silence for another minute or so. "Shanghai, do we still have any of that dynamite we stole from the army supply depot in Missouri?"

"Yep. 'Bout a half-dozen sticks."

"I think Fargo might try another raid tonight—just a hunch. But the pitcher can go once too often to the well. Let's have a little reception planned for him."

Belloch thought again about the choice blonde he would never enjoy, and his eyes went smoky with rage.

"What he pulled last night just flat out does it," he declared, his mouth stretched straight as a wire. "He's pushed me too far. From here on out, *I'm* making the medicine and that son of a bitch Fargo is taking it."

Under cover of predawn darkness Fargo approached the camp along the creek.

"Don't shoot, boys," he called out. "Fargo, riding in."

He splashed through the creek and up the grassy bank, moving into the shelter of the trees. There was enough light for him to see Dub seated on a log, the Spencer resting across his thighs.

"Decided on guard duty, eh?" he greeted the farmer.

"Yessir, two hours turnabout. That ruckus last night, when you rode out, sorta nerve-frazzled us."

"Welcome to the club." Fargo swung down and began removing the Ovaro's tack. When the leather was stripped, he led the stallion down to the creek to drink.

"Man," Dub said, "when we heard all that shooting, and then the horn blowing, we thought you was dead, Mr. Fargo. We damn near lit out of here. But without an order from you, we figured it was best to stay."

"I'm glad you did, Dub, but when you two are on your own, you don't need orders. You're in charge—you're the oldest."

Fargo led the Ovaro back into the trees. Nate rolled out of his blanket, thumbing rough crumbs of sleep from his eyes. "How's Ma and Krissy, Mr. Fargo?"

"Still pretty as four aces, both of 'em. They're taking good care of Cindy."

"Any trouble riding back in?" Dub asked. "I didn't hear no shootin'."

Fargo was briskly rubbing down the sweaty Ovaro with a feed sack. "I saw one sentry, but the idiot was asleep in the saddle. I just swung around him."

"Mr. Fargo, now that you know you can sneak out, couldn't you get that pouch to a fort?"

"Funny you should ask. I been studying on that question for a long time, but I think it's a fool's play."

"How's come?"

"Well, this jasper who held Cindy is almost surely a railroad agent, though I can't prove that right now. These cunning bastards know how low army pay is, and they buy off military clerks at any forts along the route they're trying to influence."

"The railroads stoop that low?" Nate asked. "Just break federal law bold as you please?"

"That's cast-iron fact, boy. Although, to chew it fine, it's the independent agent who does the dirt work, and he keeps the railroad in the dark about it."

"That's the fellow you named last night?" Dub said. "Bellows?"

"Belloch, according to Cindy. Anyway, they also get a civilian worker on their payroll at the forts—one who can leave at any time. A sutler, a blacksmith, a peeler—"

"They hire potato peelers?" Nate asked. "I thought soldiers did that."

Fargo laughed. "Suffer the children . . . a peeler, you punkin' roller, is a fellow who breaks green horses to leather. Now, it takes time to mount up a patrol. The clerk works in the headquarters office, so he knows immediately about any military movements."

"I get it," Dub said. "The clerk tells the worker, and the worker goes and warns the agent and his bunch. Then they clear out before the troops arrive."

"Yeah, and usually they run just the way Indians escape from the army—they keep dividing and subdividing into smaller groups and scatter to hell and gone. That leaves separate trails, and army patrols out here are usually too small to split up. So, long as you boys are still game, I say let's do this ourselves."

"I'm game," Dub declared.

"Me, too," Nate chimed in. "We gonna mount that raid tonight?"

Fargo nodded. "Last night would've been perfect—those bastards were so shellacked it would've been a turkey shoot. Now they'll be looking for us and we'll have to stay sharp."

"Let 'em look," Dub said, holding the Spencer up for emphasis. "I got a hot-lead social planned for the whole bunch."

Fargo grinned. "Pups will bark like full-growed dogs."

"I mean it, Mr. Fargo. When I looked at that girl last night, it made me hate these railroad bastards somethin' fierce."

"Railroads," Nate repeated, spitting. "Our family come out west on account everybody said a railroad was on its way. We figured that meant markets for our crops, grain exchanges and such. Still ain't no railroad, and there ain't enough water, neither. You seen our place—back in Ohio they said it was a hoeman's paradise out here, but the dirt's drier than a year-old cow chip."

"'They,'" Fargo said. "Too many pilgrims listen to 'they.' *They* are generally full of sheep dip. Besides, you came too far west. Once you pass the ninety-eighth meridian, about in the middle of the Kansas Territory, the rainfall gets dicey. Evaporation takes most of it before it reaches the ground."

"Pa never knew that," Dub said, "and he read a lot."

"I didn't get it from a book," Fargo said. "I've crossed that line dozens of times. You can look up and see rain falling toward you, but most of it doesn't make it down."

"Hell, I've seen that, too," Nate said. "I just figured my eyes was playing tricks on me."

"Anyhow," Fargo said, "the railroads don't want settlement out here just yet—not until they can control it. I've talked to farmers in the eastern part of this territory. They can't prove it, but they swear up and down that gangs like Belloch's are being hired to drive them out."

"The no 'count sons of whores," Dub said. "But what for?"

Fargo handed each boy a gnarled hunk of jerked buffalo. "So that when the tracks are finally laid, which could be anytime now unless it's delayed by a war back east, the railroad won't have to pay them compensation for their land. That's assuming, of course, that the government will recognize the settlers' claims."

"Damn. They could attack our place," Nate fretted.

"Not likely. There's not enough settlement, this far west, to make it worthwhile."

"Then what's this bunch doing here?"

"They had a specific mission," Fargo replied. "To attack the senator's fact-finding mission and prove the 'Indian menace' makes this route a bad choice. That group of Quakers was just a target of opportunity—more bloody violence to convince Congress the northern route is safer."

"Makes sense," Dub agreed. "But it makes a body's head spin to understand it. A lot of what you're saying is pure guessing, right?"

"Mostly," Fargo admitted. "But far as your place goes, I'm on solid ground there. I've seen army maps of all three proposed routes for a transcontinental railroad. One passes through Illinois and the territories way north of here. The other two cut through Kansas, but neither route puts your place in a railroad right-of-way."

By now the newborn sun was balanced like a brass coin just above the eastern horizon. Fargo had slept less than an hour at the McCallister farm and his eyelids felt weighted with coins.

"Boys," he said, stretching out in the grass with his saddle for a pillow, "I have to grab a little shut-eye. I expect our friends to try flushing us out again. You know where my spyglasses are. I want one of you up in the tree at all times, savvy?"

Both brothers nodded.

"Good. Wake me up at the first sign of trouble."

Fargo, weary to the core of his bones, fell almost immediately into a deep sleep. In his pleasant dream, he was stretched out beside the bathing pool, first Krissy, then Rosario, bouncing up and down atop him in wanton abandon.

*Mr. Fargo!*

The women kept changing places as if by magic, and the confusion didn't bother Fargo one bit. Then something began to shake his arm and Fargo started awake.

"Mr. Fargo, they're coming!"

It was Dub shaking him, and Nate was sitting up in the tree, peering through the field glasses.

"Where they at now?" Fargo said, standing up and drawing his Colt to check the loads.

"They're closing in on the spot where you shot at them yesterday—closing in slow, all spread out."

"How many riders?"

"I count fifteen or so."

"All right, here's how they'll likely play it. They're going to—Nate, careful with those glasses, they reflect—they're going to blast hell out of that spot. Soon enough they'll realize there's nobody there. Then they'll start down the creek toward us, probing."

Fargo tugged his Henry from its saddle boot and levered it to check the action.

"What are we gonna do?" Dub asked.

"You boys know what a pincers trap is?"

They both shook their heads.

Fargo said, "It's hitting your enemy from two directions at once. It works best when you have the element of surprise, which we do. Dub, bring the Spencer and throw the ammo belt over your left shoulder. Let Nate use the Colt Navy I gave you. Each of you bring your Remingtons, too."

Even as Fargo finished speaking, a blistering salvo of gunfire erupted about a mile east of them. The rapid crackle seemed to go on for at least thirty seconds.

"Tarnal hell," Dub said. "That's a right smart of guns."

"It is," Fargo agreed. "But a gun is no better than the man behind it. These jackleg 'soldiers' talk the he-bear talk, but they generally show the white feather when it comes down to the nut-cuttin'. Remember, both of you, they believe in nothing, and that means they'll save their own worthless hides if they get caught in a shit storm."

"You were right, Mr. Fargo," Nate called down. "They checked out the spot, and now they're coming toward us real slow."

"Come on down and get heeled," Fargo told him. "Here's how we play it. We'll have the advantage of both creek banks between us and them, each with its own trees and bushes. So we scoot toward them on foot just like I did yesterday. I'll station you boys at a good spot west of them. Then I'll hurry on ahead to the spot they just shot up. I'll pop out into the open and commence firing from behind them."

"Step into the *open*?" Dub repeated.

Fargo grinned. "Some say I have a trouble-seeking nature, and some might be right. But I have to let them see me to focus their attention. You two *don't* break cover, and that's a strict order. Once I start shooting, they'll whirl around to counter my attack. That's when you two complete the pincers. Nate?"

"Yessir?"

"I know you boys are both dead aims. But Dub has the rifle, and he's aiming for men. With a short gun, all you'll likely be able to plug are horses. I don't favor shooting horses when a fight is even, but the odds against us are eight to one or better if you count the whole group. And every horse you hit puts a man to flight and weakens them."

Dub looked troubled. "Won't I be shooting men in the back?"

"Back, front, it's all one target. Boy, the code out here is meant to cover two men with a grudge to settle. This is war against murderers and rapists who outnumber us. No surrender, no prisoners— if you ain't got the stomach for it, just stay here. I won't hold it against you."

When Fargo sprinted off alongside the creek, however, both boys were beside him. About a half mile east of their camp, Fargo began looking for a good spot to hide his companions.

"There," he said, pointing to the bole of a fat cottonwood. "Get across and hunker behind that tree. Soon as I open up, pour the lead to 'em. But *don't* show yourselves."

Holding his Henry at a high port, Fargo raced toward the spot from which he had ambushed the jayhawkers yesterday— the same spot they had just shot up for nothing. There was one tricky piece of work, however. He could see them through the trees, about two hundred feet past the old ambush point, and he had to slip past them unobserved.

When he was closer, Fargo dropped into the grass and rolled

rapidly, the movement made awkward by his gun belt and the rifle clutched to his chest.

A gunshot rang out, the bullet thwacking into the ground inches from his head, and Fargo froze, tasting the corroded-pennies taste of fear. Two more shots plunked into the ground, so close Fargo could feel the impact. Not only might he have been sighted, but if the boys thought that was him shooting, his plan was doomed along with the three of them.

"The hell you shooting at, Moss?"

"I think I just saw buckskins on the far bank. Can't be sure. Over in there."

"Let 'er rip, boys!" called the first voice. "Then we'll take a closer look."

Before Fargo could twitch a muscle, every man opened up— short guns, rifles, shotguns. Leaves fell on him, branches snapped, the bushes rattled as if hail were coming down. If Fargo tried to stand and flee, he knew he'd step into the path of a bullet. Instead, he made the hard decision to stay put—no man seemed to know exactly where he was.

"Cease fire!" the voice in charge commanded. "Jesus Christ, Moss, you hawg-stupid son of a bitch—your 'buckskins'! A patch of cattails!"

"Hey, Moss," jeered another voice, "the eye you got left ain't no good, neither!"

Fargo was proud of the McCallister boys. Confusing as all this must have been, they were disciplined enough to stick to the plan. He finished the distance to yesterday's ambush point, splashed through the creek, and stepped boldly out into the open.

The border ruffians were moving west. Fargo brought his notch sight between the shoulder blades of the last man and began squeezing back the trigger. "Welcome to the happy hunting grounds, scum bucket," he muttered.

The Henry spoke its piece, and the jayhawker tipped sideways out of the saddle, left foot caught in the stirrup. His panicked horse took off, the dead man bouncing up and down like a bag of rags. Fargo levered, wounded a man, levered again and missed when his target spun his horse around. By now all the border ruffians had spotted him. Just as they opened up on Fargo, however, the McCallister boys rained in a deadly storm of bullets.

Fargo stood his ground, despite the bullets snapping past him, levering and firing three more rounds. Dub had killed at least two men, and Fargo watched first a claybank, then a sorrel buckle to their knees. Then he spotted the sight he had dreaded: the jay-hawker leader called Moss, bringing his Big Fifty to the ready.

Fargo dove headlong into the tree cover as the big-caliber gun boomed. At the same time a panicked voice screamed out repeatedly: "Retreat, damn it, retreat!" By the time Fargo got to his feet, the badly shot-up men were thundering toward their camp, several seriously wounded jayhawkers hunched over in the saddle.

The two men in the grass had sustained hits to the head and required no finishing shots. The one Fargo killed was still bouncing across the plains full chisel, his debt to society paid in full.

Fargo sprinted toward the brothers' position. "Fancy-fine shooting, boys! I'll guarandamntee you they won't play pheasant flush with us anymore."

"Mr. Fargo!" Dub's nearly hysterical voice replied. "Hurry! Nate's been hit, and there's a powerful lot of blood!"

# 11

Fargo's first thought, when he heard Dub's calamitous words, was, *Damn! Nate's a good kid, but I put him in over his head*. His second thought, however, was even more troubling: *If Nate dies, you're honor-bound to take him home to his mother*. Fargo would rather harrow hell and deliver a Bible to the devil than return a dead son to his mother.

"Hurry, Mr. Fargo!" Dub pleaded as the Trailsman reached his position. "Hurry!"

"All right, I'm here, Dub, get reloads in your rifle, then watch to the east in case those bastards about-face on us."

Nate lay writhing in the grass, breathing hard like a woman in labor.

"Where you hit, son?" Fargo said, kneeling beside him. "Belly? Chest?"

"My leg," Nate gasped. "Left leg."

"Your . . . ?" Fargo bit his lower lip to keep a straight face. There was a small trace of blood on the ankle of his grain-sack trousers.

"It's curtains for me, Mr. Fargo," he said dramatically. "No need to sugarcoat it. I'm a gone beaver, ain't I?"

Fargo slit the pant leg with his toothpick and glanced at the wound. "Boy, get straight with your Maker. You're about bled out."

"I knew it," Nat wailed. "You hear that, Dub? Gunned down on the plains. Just like in *Wild West Adventures*."

"That's right, boy," Fargo said. "Nobody can call you piss-proud now. You're a fighting frontiersman, and your name will go down with Caleb Greenwood, Jim Bridger, and Daniel Boone."

"Can't you save him, Mr. Fargo?" Dub pleaded from behind him.

Fargo finally had to take pity on Dub. "Save him from *what*, you damn young fools? There ain't enough blood here to feed a baby skeeter."

"What? He ain't shot up bad?"

"Dub, the boy ain't even *shot*. I've wounded myself worse just shaving. He got grazed along the ankle, is all, just like I got grazed in the neck yesterday. Prob'ly a ricochet. It's piddlin'. Take a look."

Dub bent over his brother, then flushed to the roots of his tow hair. "Christ, Nate, you damn weak sister! Way you carried on, I thought you was dying."

Fargo forced himself not to laugh. "Never mind. It's still a bullet wound, after all, and a man's first time is apt to rattle him. I'm just glad he's all right. And the main mile is that you two fellows did some fine shooting. C'mon, Nate."

Fargo helped him up. "I'll put some salve on it and wrap it with a strip of linen."

"You little she-male," Dub muttered. "'It's curtains for me.' That ain't nothing but a rope burn."

"Kiss my hinder," Nate retorted. "*You* ain't never been shot."

They returned to their simple camp and Fargo tended to the leg. By now both boys were starting to realize they had been in their first shooting scrape—and acquitted themselves well.

"Any regrets?" Fargo asked them.

"You kidding? It beats the Dutch," Nate replied.

"Caps the climax," Dub added. "It ain't like we shot up decent men. I think I'm gonna be a sheriff—maybe even a U.S. marshal."

"Don't go off half-cocked," Fargo warned. "This today was an ambush, with the element of surprise on our side. Last night, in their camp, they were corned. But we can't count on Old Churnbrain tonight."

"These men sure *look* tough," Dub said. "How's come we run 'em off so easy just now?"

"Don't get cocky," Fargo warned. "They can be trouble when they want to be. They were smart to hightail it just now. They were caught in a pincers, and that was their own stupid fault. These old boys are too lazy to learn trail craft and tactics. They may look tough, Dub, but the truth is they're hard."

"What's the difference?" Nate asked.

"Well, this bunch is what you might call easy-go killers. For them murder is as natural as taking a leak. That makes them dangerous—real dangersome, as Old Jules would put it. But only when the odds are with them because, at heart, they're cowards like most criminals. But never forget they're dangerous—and when they're cornered, like rats, they fight."

At regular intervals Fargo climbed up into the cottonwood and checked the plains all around them. He spotted one or two isolated riders, but no one came close to the creek.

"I wish we could start a cooking fire," Nate complained early in the afternoon. "This hardtack and jerky are hard to swallow."

"Soak the hardtack in water," Fargo suggested. "That way the weevils float to the top and you can pick 'em out. Then you can just eat the rest with a spoon."

The two brothers looked at each other and seemed on the verge of puking.

"There's weevils in it?" Nate demanded.

Fargo laughed. "The hell you think flavors it? Anyhow, we can build a pit fire after dark and stoke our bellies for the raid."

"Good." Dub hooked a thumb toward the opposite bank. "I made a snare, and there's a big rabbit caught in it. I brained it with a rock."

Fargo broke out his deck of cards and resumed the brothers' poker lessons, teaching them the fine art of bluffing. The afternoon heated up, and now and then the horses stamped their feet in vexation at pesky flies.

"Mr. Fargo," Nate said, mulling a hand of cards, "do you think me and Dub is good enough aims to be gunfighters?"

Gunfighter. That was a new term Fargo had first heard applied to the California bandit Joaquin Murrieta, a fast-draw artist who carried a French cap-and-ball pistol in his sash for quick use. Now everybody and his mother was billed a "gunfighter."

"Listen," he said, "don't let your fine aim trick you into thinking you're quick on the draw. They're two separate skills. Just remember there's no second place in a gunfight—you win or you die."

"You been in some?"

"I've avoided more than I've been in, and I'm damned if I'll ruin my holster by oiling it. There's more talk about them than actual gunfights."

"Can't be that much to pulling a gun out of a holster," Dub opined.

"Well, I'm no gunslick," Fargo said, standing up. "But now you two have gun belts, so let's test your draw. You first, Dub. Make sure your gun ain't cocked. Go ahead—skin it back."

Dub was still clearing leather when the muzzle of Fargo's Colt was aimed dead center on his torso. Nate fared no better.

"Damnation," Nate said as they resumed their game. "It's like it just jumps into your hand."

"Yeah, well, if that impresses you, remember this—I'm slow compared to a professional gunfighter."

"Couldn't you be one if you wanted to?" Dub asked.

"Why would I want to? A gunfighter is a board walker in town. Spends hours every day practicing his draw in hotel mirrors, like some woman fussing over her hair. He depends on restaurants for his meals, stores for his clothes, and he makes his money doing other men's killing for them. Just like this bunch we're up against now."

"It don't sound like no way to live," Dub admitted. "Pa use to say that a real man goes to bed every night with a clean conscience."

"Damn straight. And you never hear of these gunmen living to old age. Dealer takes three," Fargo said, slapping down his discards. "Say, what's all this talk of gunfighters and marshaling? What's wrong with being a man like your father was?"

"Nothing," Dub said. "But he was just a farmer. You have adventures."

"I'm just a drifter, and all drifters run into adventures. But it takes one hell of a man to work himself to death for his family. It's natural for young men like you to want to see the elephant. But consider honest work. The West needs scouts, hunters, drovers, soldiers, boatmen, teamsters—you'll have adventures in any of those jobs, and you won't have to sit with your back to a wall, waiting for some seedy killer to paper the room with your brains."

"Yeah, I wouldn't mind being a scout for the army," Nate said. "And you've taught us some tricks already. But how does a man get good enough to get hired on?"

"You have to trot before you can canter," Fargo assured him. "Speaking of which, I know you boys are fond of your farm nags. But they're placing you at risk out here. You need horses that can gallop and run."

"How you plan to wangle that?" Dub asked.

"How else? I'm going to liberate two saddle horses from the jayhawkers."

"But you told us outlaws' horses are abused," Nate reminded him, staring at his cards as if they'd betrayed him.

Fargo nodded. "They've been spurred up bad and rode hard and put away wet so much that most have saddle sores. But these dobbins will get you killed."

Dub said, "Do we have to shoot 'em?"

"I never said that. We'll just leave them hidden in the trees for now. I can't guarantee their survival, but hell, I can't guarantee our survival."

"Is this going to be tonight?" Dub asked.

"I called one-eyed jacks wild," Fargo reminded him. "Don't toss it into the deadwood, pick it up and play it. Yeah, tonight. I noticed last night they only keep one guard at the rope corral. You two will wait with your dobbins out on the plains. I'll do for the guard and pick you out two horses. After we picket them with your farm horses, we go back and give the camp a lead bath. To make sure they don't catch us, I'll leave the corral open. The racket of gunfire will scatter the mounts."

"Them killers will be waiting for us tonight, huh?" Dub asked.

"As sure as cats fighting. But it's best to keep 'em rattled. We've poured it to 'em two days in a row down here by the creek, and night before last I powder-burned two of them in the oak grove. By now they know the death hug's a-comin', and these are not men willing to sacrifice—they're cold-blooded murderers in it to win it—for themselves. Your deal, Nate."

Fargo paused to recall Cindy's words about the leader of the border ruffians: *After he buttoned my dress back up, he whispered in my ear, "Life is a disease, and the only cure is death."*

"What is it, Mr. Fargo?" Dub asked, watching his face.

"I was just thinking how queer it is. We've had plenty of set-tos with this bunch, but we still haven't laid eyes on the biggest toad in the puddle."

Throughout the afternoon Fargo climbed the cottonwood to keep an eye on their enemy. But the only activity was an isolated rider or two heading into Sublette. Near the end of the afternoon a freight wagon pulled by six big dray horses rumbled up to the trading post.

Dub was busy cleaning the Spencer carbine. "See anything, Mr. Fargo?"

"Nothing we need to worry about. A pair of jayhawkers rode to a saloon, but most seem to be staying at their camp."

"Waiting for us," Nate said.

"The way you say," Fargo agreed. "This won't be like the magazines you read. You could get killed. We all could. Are you certain-sure you want to do this?"

"I know Pa would have," Nate said. "That's good enough for me."

"Me, too," Dub added. "These sons of bitches are trying to kill us."

"Stout lads."

Fargo hung from the lowest limb and dropped to the ground. The McCallister boys' faces looked brassy in the fading sunlight.

"Almost time to knock up some grub," he said. "Nate, dress out that rabbit and spit it. I'll lay a fire."

Fargo scooped out their fire pit even deeper and piled up dried grass and crumbled bark for kindling. He was out of lucifer matches, so he removed the flint and steel from his possibles bag. When the sun finally blazed out on the western horizon, he struck sparks until the kindling was ablaze, then piled small chunks of dead branches onto the flames.

Rabbit meat got too greasy if it was actually cooked, so Fargo just quickly scorched it and divided the food up.

"Before we leave," he said, chewing the hot meat, "make sure you've got six beans in the wheels of your handguns. Dub, stick to the Spencer and reserve one short gun for any close-in trouble. Nate, that trade rifle won't be worth a kiss-my-ass for this fandango tonight, so just leave it behind. Empty one handgun and keep the other in reserve for any trouble on the retreat, savvy that?"

"Yessir," both boys replied in unison.

"Good. I'll steal the horses while you boys wait. Then I'll post you. *Retreat on your own* as soon as you're down to your reserve gun. Try not to throw any lead until I open fire, but the second you hear my Henry cracking, wake snakes, hear?"

Fargo let those orders sink in before adding the rest: "Nighttime shoot-outs are confusing, and we want maximum firepower to scare them into thinking there's more than three of us. And speaking of nighttime, remember that your muzzle flash gives them a target. So move a few feet to a new spot after every two shots."

Fargo wiped his hands in the grass. "One more thing. I don't count on many kills tonight, if any. They won't have big fires burning, and they won't likely be drunk. This raid is mostly to harass them and convince the drones to desert their leaders."

Fargo glanced overhead and saw the branches making cracks in the moon. The talking part of it was over. Now came the hard doing.

"Time to raise dust," he said. "Now, I need a promise from both of you."

"Yessir?" Dub said.

"Just this. I never plan on getting killed or shot up bad, but if it happens, I want you boys to hightail it back to camp. Don't wait for me."

"You'd wait for us," Dub objected.

"You miss my point. I do want you to save your hides, but also, that pouch *can't* fall into their hands. Somebody has to deliver it to the soldiers. My horse is used to you boys now and considers you friends. He'll follow you on a lead line. He's yours if I don't make it out. But promise you'll retreat and deliver that pouch."

"Promise," Dub said reluctantly.

"Me, too," Nate said.

"All right. Make sure you bring your blankets along, I'll show you another scouting trick. Let's go raise some hell."

Despite a bright full moon, dense clouds darkened the plains, which Fargo took as a good omen. They trotted their mounts due east, Fargo enforcing strict silence. About halfway to the motte of pines, Fargo told the boys to wrap their heads as he did.

"Jehosaphat!" Nate whispered when they removed their blankets. "It's like dusk instead of dead of night."

"Make sure to *use* that advantage," Fargo admonished, forking leather. "Try not to look into any fires or you'll lose it."

"I won't. Man, Dub, we're learning some slick tricks from—"

"Stow it," Fargo snapped. "This is what the army calls movement to contact phase—the most dangerous time. *No* talk that isn't necessary. Just look and listen."

From here the trio held their horses to a walk, Fargo guessing that, on such a dark night, their enemy might be listening. He circled around to the north side this time and reined in a quarter mile from the dark mass of trees.

All three hobbled their mounts. The boys held back while Fargo moved quickly forward in spurts, relying on his mind map to guide him toward the rope corral at the edge of the outer ring of trees.

He had guessed correctly: the jayhawkers, expecting trouble, had built no fires tonight. But Fargo's enhanced night vision, and their glowing pipes and cigarettes, allowed him to make out small groups of men. He spotted the milling horses and started to duck under one of the ropes.

The metallic click of a gun being cocked, just inches from his head, made Fargo's bowels go loose and heavy with dread. But he reacted with lightning-fast reflexes, filling his hand and smashing the barrel of his Colt downward hard on the sentry's temple, knocking him unconscious and unhinging his knees—the same quick "buffalo" blow that had saved Fargo's life several times before.

Fargo's blade cut deep and wide into the man's throat to finish him off. He wiped the blade off on the corpse's pants and moved into the corral. The horses whiffed the stallion smell on him, and only a few bothered to nicker. Still, it was enough noise to cause notice.

"Jubilee!" an authoritative voice rang out from the camp. "Them horses all right?"

"Rabbit spooked 'em," Fargo called back.

"Yeah? Well, just keep your eyes peeled. You already let that son of a bitch slip past you once."

Fargo picked two of the friendliest, best-muscled horses, both geldings, a sorrel and a black with no white markings. The tack was heaped in a corner, so he tossed a saddle and bridle on each mount, then cut the rope on the side of the corral facing the open plains, keeping the cut rope.

"Boys, your new horses," he greeted the McCallister brothers. "Tie lead lines to your nags, then let's get this medicine show on the road."

He cut the rope into two pieces and gave one to each youth.

"Now remember," he told them, "wait till I shoot. As soon as you're down to six bullets in reserve, retreat to your horses and head back to camp."

Soon the three men were sneaking into the outer pines. Relying on his mental map, Fargo posted Nate on his left, Dub on his right, each with a tree to cover him. Fargo took up his own position and aimed at a dark mass of men straight ahead.

His first shot shattered the silence and unleashed a hammering of gunfire from his companions. But this time their enemy was ready, and the return firepower was even more intense. Rifles, handguns, and scatterguns opened up from the inner rings of trees, and because Fargo had fired first, his position drew most of the lead—just as he had planned.

Branches snapped, pine needles rained down, and splinters of wood turned the air dangerous. Fargo levered and fired, moving quickly to a new tree after every pair of shots. Somebody on his team had struck pay dirt—a border ruffian howled in pain.

Fargo felt a flood of relief when he heard the horses scattering. He doubted that this bunch would pursue him and the boys on foot, across open plains, to the horses, nor could they chase them in the saddle. They would spend the rest of the night, and probably much of tomorrow, rounding up their horses.

Bullets whiffed past him so close that he felt the wind-rip on his cheeks. The boys had ceased fire, and Fargo hoped that meant they were retreating. Fortunately, none of the sixteen bullets in his Henry hung fire, and when he heard the hammer fall on an empty chamber, Fargo turned to run.

And that's when everything went drastically wrong.

*"Aye!"* a voice shouted behind him. "I hear him! Throw it straight ahead!"

Fargo heard a sickeningly familiar sound: the fizzling and crackling of a fuse. He put on an extra burst of speed, but in midstride a dangerously close explosion lit up the night and slammed into him like a mule kick.

The blast heaved him into the air as Skye Fargo's world shut down to darkness.

# 12

*Grab him under his armpit, Nate! Space your shots out!*

Fargo felt himself bumping roughly along the ground as he fought to swim up from the murky depths of unconsciousness. Guns were barking close to his ears, and shots filled the air.

*Christ, here they come! Make every bullet score, Nate!*

Fargo's eyes snapped open, and he smelled singed hair. Somebody was dragging him across the grassy plain.

"Shit-oh-dear!" he heard Dub shout. "They're rushing us, brother. I'm down to two shots!"

"I'm out!"

Fargo, still too weak to fight loose, slapped leather and fired at the shadows chasing them—six accurately placed shots that broke the jayhawkers' bravado and sent them back into the tree cover.

"Way to hold and squeeze, Mr. Fargo!" Dub exclaimed. "We thought you was dead."

Even as he was dragged along, Fargo, battle-hardened by experience, began thumbing reloads into the wheel of his Colt in case of another charge.

"I think I can stand up now, fellows. Reload your short guns."

They pulled Fargo, still woozy and disoriented, to his feet. Each youth reloaded, then took an arm and helped Fargo back to the horses.

"You hurt bad?" Dub asked.

Fargo carefully checked every body part. "The bastards singed my beard, is all. Eyebrows are gone, too, but I held on to my rifle."

"Criminy, they got dynamite," Nate said.

"Yeah, but we poured it to 'em good, buddy," Dub boasted.

"Caulk up, both of you," Fargo snapped. "This is no time to recite our coups. The enemy could still attack while we're retreating. Watch our backtrail close."

Fargo's warning rang true when, a heartbeat later, a shower of orange sparks came arcing toward them. Fargo put a bear hug round both boys and drove them to the left as an earsplitting explosion showered them with dirt and grass.

"Open fire dead ahead!" Fargo ordered, Colt jumping in his fist.

A group of jayhawkers had rushed forward under cover of the explosion, but three six-guns spitting lead persuaded them to retreat.

"This is the last time we try this play," Fargo said as the trio mounted, Dub and Nate holding lead lines. "These sons of trouble are getting desperate."

They spotted a few of the liberated horses, contentedly grazing, as they rode west to their camp.

"How's them new mounts?" Fargo asked.

"This sorrel's fine," Dub said. "Real comfortable gait. I'm not used to a real saddle, though."

"That saddle will have to shape to your horse's back," Fargo said. "I just grabbed two off the pile."

"This black's all right, too," Nate said. "Seems a mite skittish, is all."

"Most outlaws' horses are," Fargo said. "He's expecting the spurs."

They reached camp safely and stripped the leather from their mounts after watering them and placing them on long tethers. Fargo gave each of the brothers a horseshoe nail.

"These will work as hoof picks. Once a day," he told them, "check a horse's hooves for stones. Once a stone crack works its way up the fetlock, a horse is ruined."

"Damnation, Mr. Fargo," Nate exalted. "We done pretty good tonight, huh? Got two horses, set the rest free, and shot the hell outta their camp."

"You boys will do to take along," Fargo agreed. "You proved me wrong. You do have the caliber for this job."

The brothers looked at each other, and even in the dim light Fargo could see their ear-to-ear smiles.

"There's one problem," Fargo added, making his voice solemn.

"What?" they both demanded.

"You made a promise to me to retreat no matter what happened to me. You gave your word, and you broke it. A man's word is his bond."

"Yessir," Dub muttered.

"Well, that's grave, lads. And . . ." Fargo paused dramatically. "I'm mighty glad you broke your word. Hell, I owe my life to you gutsy sons of bucks."

The McCallister boys, not expecting this, stared at Fargo.

"Boys, when that dynamite blew me into the air, I thought I'd bought the farm, bull and all."

"But what do we do next?" Dub asked. "You said we can't attack their camp no more."

Fargo spread his groundsheet, then his blanket. "I'll have to study on that. I know this much: Belloch wants that pouch bad, and if we don't come up with a plan, our enemy will."

The situation at the border ruffians' camp was critical, and Rafe Belloch knew it. Twice now Fargo and his young sidekicks had repelled attacks along the creek, with bloody results for the jay-hawkers. And twice Fargo had slipped, seemingly at will, into their camp. Add to that the two killings in the cottonwood grove, of Les and Harney, and the men were on the verge of total desertion—assuming they all found their horses.

Last night's attack, Belloch told himself, was more noisy than it was deadly. With the grisly exception of Jubilee Lofley, whose head was half severed from his neck, only two men had been wounded. But these men were badly spooked now, and only a drastic change in tactics might hold them together.

"Gents," he addressed his three lieutenants, "you may *think* our tits are caught in a wringer, but I assure you—Fargo needn't be tacking up bunting just yet. Not by a jugful."

Shanghai, Moss, and Jake sat at the deal table, watching their employer pace.

"The hell you jabbering about, Mr. Belloch?" Jake demanded. "What's bunting?"

Belloch stared at the sullen, terrier-faced lackey until he glanced away. This was a new tone from Jake, and Belloch warned himself that he could lose all control over these piggish killers if he tolerated rebellion.

"I don't know, boss," Shanghai said. "Him and them tads with him has put damn near ten of our men out of the fight, counting the wounded we've had to kill. It sure *seems* like our tits are caught in a wringer."

Rafe waved a negligent hand. "Never mind those ten—their bones will raise *our* throne higher. I'll divide their pay among the rest. I tell you, *we* will live to piss on Fargo's grave."

"Yeah, but you know these men," Moss said. "They been pushed to their limit. Right now it's two hours past sunup, and half of them are still trying to catch their horses. If we're lucky they'll just light a shuck back to the eastern territory. If we're unlucky, they'll kill us all for our money."

"It won't come to that," Rafe insisted. "By now our report, framing Fargo for that attack on the Quakers, has reached the military."

"No offense, boss," Shanghai said. "But you add that report to a nail, and you'll have a nail. Who knows how long before they look into it. There's rumors of war brewing back east, and the frontier forts are down to just enough soldiers for force protection. But Fargo works fast. It ain't even been a week since we locked horns with him, yet the cockchafer has done the hurt dance on us."

"You're right, Shanghai, the man has an endless supply of fox plays. But our mistake has been in trying to beat him at field tactics. We should have been using wit and wile."

"How so?"

Rafe gazed out the open front of the dugout, hands clasped behind him. "We've been looking for a chink in Fargo's armor, right? Well, I think I know of one."

He turned around. "Moss, the other night you said that if Rosario had set you up to be killed, as she did with Fargo, you'd have gutted her."

The one-eyed redhead nodded. "Yeah, after I bulled her a couple times."

"Me, too," Jake cut in. "She's got tits. I'd like to—"

"Jake," Shanghai cut him off, "your mouth runs like a whippoor-will's ass. Shut the hell up."

"Killing her is how any of us would have handled it," Rafe continued. "After pondering it, I'm not sure Fargo really beat her as Shanghai reported. That damage could have been artfully contrived. But let's assume Fargo did beat her—why didn't he kill her?"

"Because he wanted to poke her again?" Jake guessed.

Sudden anger and annoyance darkened Belloch's gaze. "Jake, you have a remarkable knack for grasping the obvious and missing the essence. He didn't kill her, you ignorant chawbacon, because he lives by a code of honor. And it's that code we'll use to bring him down."

"I'm sick and tired of all your damn insults," Jake complained.

"Do tell?"

Jake's words fairly tumbled over each other in his pent-up need to make his case. "Yessir, I will tell. Our hash is cooked, Mr. Belloch, and it's all your fault. Jubilee makes it nine that has died now, and number ten is dyin' as we speak. We didn't lose this many in the Lawrence raid. We need to pull up stakes before Fargo kills the rest of us. You act like king coyote, but all your fancy plans ain't worth a shit."

A lethal sense of purpose concentrated Belloch's features. "That's mighty tall talk, Ketchum."

"Like hell it is. You talk like a book, all right, but you been wrong all along about Fargo. He hangs on like a tick, and if we stay here we're in for six sorts of hell. You'll catch a weasel asleep before you kill him. Truth be told, you're just a damn little barber's clerk. Ain't never killed a man in your life, not with your own hands."

"You mean . . . like this?"

Not one of the three men had seen Belloch tug the Spanish dagger out of his boot. In one fast, hard snap it flew across the dugout and straight into Jake's throat, burying itself deep. He managed to lurch to his feet, making a ghastly choking noise, then hit the dirt floor with a sound like a sack of salt landing on hardpan. His heels scratched several times before he died.

"He was a bird-brained idiot," Belloch announced calmly. "Not worth a fart in a whirlwind. I'll keep him on the payroll and split his share between you two."

"Damn, boss, you're some pumpkins with that dagger," Shanghai said. "Savage as a meat ax! Hope you ain't plannin' the same for us."

"Rest easy, gents. You've both been a strong right arm to me, and I'm glad you nailed your colors to my mast. Jake, however, got on my nerves, the ignorant mudsill. He was even stupider than God made him."

Now Rafe played his ace. He pulled out his money purse and gave each man eighty dollars in gold.

"Hell," Moss said, "it's no say-so of Jake's what you do. You done the hiring."

"And now I've done the firing."

"So what do you have in mind for Rosario?" Shanghai asked.

"Ahh," Belloch replied. "As to that . . ."

Throughout the morning and afternoon following the strike on the jayhawker camp, Fargo and the McCallister boys maintained tight vigilance. One of them stayed up in the tree at all times, and Fargo frequently felt the ground with three fingertips to detect large groups of riders.

"This is boring," Nate said toward the middle of the afternoon. "That set-to last night got my blood to singing."

Fargo, busy oiling the Henry's lever mechanism, gave that remark a sardonic grin. "When you're a little older, you'll appreciate being bored."

"They could still attack," Dub called down from the tree. "Plenty of daylight left."

"They could, but I can't see it," Fargo gainsaid. "They haven't fared too well in these last two scrapes along the creek. And along about now, if I know these border thugs, they're starting to sull on their leaders. This Belloch is likely having some trouble putting down a mutiny."

"You got a plan yet?" Nate asked.

"I'm hanged if I do. It's been six days now since these sage rats attacked the Quakers, and now we're boxed in here. It's dragging out too long, and time usually favors the larger force."

"'Cept if they mutiny, right?"

"That would change things," Fargo conceded. "But exactly how is anybody's guess. They might kill Belloch. But the railroad didn't hire him because he's stupid. We already know he's got lickfingers higher up the payroll like Shanghai Webb and this fellow Moss—the one with the Big Fifty. I'd guess the main gather will soon be paid off and ride back east, and Belloch and his ramrods will just hire new men from Sublette. That, or they'll clear out."

"But first he has to get that pouch, right?" Dub asked. "I mean, before he leaves these parts?"

"As sure as sun in the morning," Fargo said. "And I'd wager he's working on that plan right now."

Fargo took the next stint up in the tree. About thirty minutes into his watch, he lifted the field glasses to his eyes and saw a line of riders heading south from the trading post.

Below him, the McCallister boys were in a heated dispute over a poker game.

"Damn your hide, Nate!" Dub snapped. "Mr. Fargo said you can't peek at the deadwood."

"Like hell he did! He said you're not supposed to look at the discard pile, but it wasn't considered cheating."

"Stow the chin-wag, boys," Fargo cut in. "We've got riders, and I don't believe what I'm seeing."

"What?" they chimed in unison, throwing down their cards.

But Fargo was speechless with growing rage and didn't bother to answer them. The riders had turned west, paralleling the creek but staying out of easy rifle range. He saw Shanghai Webb leading the pack—and holding a pistol to the head of the lead rider, whose hands were bound behind her.

Fargo recognized the woman as Rosario—and the jayhawkers had stripped her buck.

When Fargo failed to answer them, the brothers had raced across the creek to the opposite bank to peer out from the tree cover. After a few minutes, as the riders drew closer to their position, Dub exclaimed: "Why, it's a sin to Crockett! They got a woman prisoner, and—and it looks like she's naked as a jay!"

"That's Rosario," Fargo told them. "And if you had spyglasses, you'd see she's not just naked—she's scared to death."

"Can we look through the spyglasses?" Nate pleaded.

"No. You think this is a saloon show for your entertainment?"

"*You're* looking. I ain't never seen a naked woman 'cept for Krissy, and your sister don't count."

She does if she's *not* your sister, Fargo thought.

"Shut pan, Nate," Dub snapped. "What are they up to, Mr. Fargo?"

"Well, we were just talking about it. I'd wager this is Belloch's plan to get that pouch."

"You mean, Rosario for the pouch?"

"What else? He ain't passing her in review just for our entertainment."

"Hell, I can't see much anyhow," Nate complained. "They're near a mile off."

"But why is she naked?" Dub pressed. "It don't make no sense."

In memory Fargo heard Cindy's exhausted voice: *Skye, he said my black eye had to fade first. He said, "I don't poke bruised fruit."*

"Because Belloch's a sick, disgusting son of a bitch, that's why," Fargo replied. "It's his way of telling us she'll be raped by every one of his men before she's killed."

"You gonna do it, Mr. Fargo?" Dub asked. "Trade, I mean. When you saved Cindy, you said a feller is honor-bound to save a woman."

"He is, but you have to bend with the breeze or you'll break. We have to see how those jackals play this, boys. But I'll tell you this right now—no deals with the devil. This bunch has no plan to honor any terms they offer."

The riders stopped at a spot parallel to the place where Fargo had twice ambushed them.

"They still think we're holed up down there," he said. "And Belloch must be holding this bunch together somehow—he wants us to see that. There's at least fifteen riders out there."

"Is he with them, you think?" Dub asked.

"Not unless he's a scruffy-looking owlhoot wearing filthy rags, and that's not how Cindy described him—she makes him sound like a dandy, Besides, his kind don't like to show themselves. Say . . . what's this?"

Fargo watched the redhead called Moss ride out a few yards and ram a pointed stake into the ground. What looked like a sheet of paper had been tied to the top with a rawhide string.

"What's goin' on?" Nate demanded. "We can't see much."

"There's a note on that stake," Fargo replied. "It likely lays down Belloch's terms. I pretty much know what it says."

"They're riding back toward Sublette now," Nate said. "You want me to ride out and get the note?"

"Nix on that, you young fool. It's still broad daylight. This could all be an elaborate trap to trick us into revealing our real camp. I'll ride out after dark."

The sun was westering, the day hot and almost windless. Fargo broke out three more strips of jerky from the dwindling supply in his saddlebag. They spent the rest of the day cooling off in the creek, moving the horses to fresh graze, and taking turns on guard duty up in the tree.

Two hours after sunset Fargo deemed it dark enough to ride out. He tacked the Ovaro and cantered out to the stake, spotting it easily because of the moonlight reflecting off the white foolscap. Back at camp he built a small fire in the pit and read the missive out loud to the boys:

"'Fargo: My compliments. I realize now that the talk about you is not just pub lore.'"

"What's pub mean?" Nate interrupted.

"Saloon. 'You have something I want, and I have something to barter in exchange. Tomorrow, at noon, my men will ride back out with the girl. To prove my good faith, they will meet you halfway between the stake and the creek. You may bring your weapons along with the pouch, and *all* of my men will have their hands up where you can see them. We know you are deadly, and if we try to double-cross you, you will kill many of us. Once you hand over the pouch, Rosario is yours. If you reject my offer, she will die a dog's death as will you and your young friends. Accept it, however, and the war between us is over.' He didn't sign the note."

"You think he's on the level?" Dub asked.

"So what if he is? Like I said, no deals with the devil."

"But Rosario—"

"Stick your 'butts' back in your pocket. It's past peace-piping now," Fargo insisted. "We'll save Rosario if we can, but not if it means letting more people be killed and raped. We're going to try to save her, all right, but Belloch doesn't get that pouch while I'm still above the horizon. There's only one reason he wants it so bad—because it's the gallows for him if it's ever handed over to soldiers."

Fargo read the note again, and his lips slid back off his teeth in a wolfish grin.

"What?" Dub demanded.

"Do you remember when the three of us walked into the trading post, and Nate mistook a faro game for poker?"

"Uh-hunh. So did I."

"Well . . . there were jayhawkers there, and it got back to Belloch that I'm sided by a couple of rube farm boys. They know

I've got two young partners who ride plow nags. But they don't know yet that you two are dead shots."

"What about that shoot-out yesterday, down the creek," Nate pointed out. "We give 'em what for."

"You sure's hell did, but that was at close range, and they were caught in a pincers. They can't know what hit 'em. My point is, these fools are scared of me but don't realize you two are dangerous shooters. That's why they're offering to meet me halfway. And halfway puts them right in your sights."

"For us it's close," Dub agreed.

"Close enough for you two shootists to make my Henry and that Spencer sing a death song," Fargo agreed. "And here's how us three are gonna play this hand . . ."

Just past noon on the following day, Fargo spotted the same riders from yesterday bearing toward them in single file from the direction of Sublette. He and the McCallister brothers had already moved east to the decoy spot where the jayhawkers thought they were holed up.

"Here's the fandango," Fargo said, peering through his glasses. "At least Rosario is dressed today."

"Aww," Nate said, his disappointment keen.

"Would you want to be buck naked with all these flies and skeeters biting you, shitheel?" Dub demanded.

"Nobody wants to see a man naked, knothead," Nate shot back.

"Both of you cinch your lips," Fargo snapped. "Make a last check of your weapons. My ass will be hanging in the breeze out there, and if you two gum up the works, me and Rosario will be shot to sieves."

Fargo studied the opposition closer. Rosario again had her wrists bound behind her, but he noted thankfully that her ankles were not tied. The tight stays of her red dress thrust her breasts up prominently.

The deadly caravan stopped opposite them, several hundred yards out.

"Well, they got their hands up—for now," Nate said. "I think they mean to cut you down when you're close enough, Mr. Fargo."

"So do I, Nate," Fargo agreed. "That's why timing is everything. You two just keep an eye out for my signal. Watch for the main chance—it won't come twice. Dub, you shoot from the head of the column toward the middle. Nate, you start in the middle and shoot toward the end. One bullet, one jayhawker."

Fargo picked up a saddlebag. The pouch was in the one he left behind.

"Well, it's time to call in the cards, boys. I hope I remember the right Spanish word," he added by way of farewell as he stepped into the clear.

Fargo felt like a bull's-eye on a target, one that grew bigger as he drew nearer. His right hand rested on the butt of his Colt, and he kept a vigilant eye on all those raised hands—especially on Shanghai Webb's and the sharpshooting weasel called Moss.

"Here comes the big crusader, boys," Shanghai called to the rest when Fargo was within earshot. "He won't bag no quail withouten he's got *permission*. Ain't that sweet and noble?"

Derisive laughter echoed across the plains.

"*Cuidado*, Fargo," Rosario warned. "*Es una trampa.*"

Fargo already knew it was a trap. Shanghai cuffed her so hard she slid sideways in the saddle.

"No more of that goddamn greaser talk," he growled, "or I'll burn you where you sit."

Just a little closer, Fargo thought. Just twenty more feet.

"You even *try* to clear leather," Fargo warned him, "and I'll sink an air shaft through you."

"You best wise up, Fargo. The second you jerk back that shooter, you'll have a wall of lead pouring into you."

"Won't do *you* any good, will it, Shanghai? How many of your roaches have I already stepped on?"

Fargo didn't expect the play to come from Shanghai, but from one of the men behind him. But Shanghai was the worst threat to Rosario. The moment Fargo figured he was close enough, he said in an amiable, conversational tone, "Rosario, *subate ahora*." At the same time, Fargo reached up as if tipping his hat to her— the prearranged signal to the boys.

Fargo's Spanish was good enough for Rosario to take his meaning—she instantly slid off the right side of the horse, land- ing in an ungainly heap on the ground. Before she even hit the grass, Shanghai's head exploded in a spray of blood and pebbly brain matter.

# 13

The horse Rosario had been riding panicked and reared up. Fargo raced forward, threw himself on the frightened woman, and rolled with her to safety just before the gelding brought its sharp, pointed hoofs down where she had landed.

Fargo shucked out his Colt, searching for Moss and his deadly Big Fifty. But the astounding marksmanship of the McCallister boys had negated all resistance. With at least four dead or dying border ruffians bleeding into the plains, and several more twisted into their saddles with wounds, the rest were scattering to the east like scalded dogs.

"You all right?" Fargo asked Rosario as he sliced through her ropes and helped her up.

"My *hombro*," she replied, rubbing her shoulder, "is sore from the fall. But, Skye Fargo, I am so happy to be alive. *Thank you*."

"Well, you should really thank those two boys," Fargo said. "Damn but they can shoot. Speaking of that . . . turn your back."

One of the jayhawkers had been shot through the neck and was choking in his own blood. Fargo tossed a finishing shot into his brain, then tugged the shell belts off the dead men, leaving three of the five handguns—they had enough hardware to haul around already. Fargo could have used one more good rifle, but all the riderless horses had followed the others.

"Where will I stay now?" Rosario asked as they began walking back to the tree line. "I dare not return to the trading post."

"You won't be too comfortable," Fargo replied, "but you'll have to stay with us for at least a day. That'll give me time to see what this bunch has done. We've killed half their men now. I predict that the rest will light out today."

"Light out?" she repeated. *"Que quiere decir?"*

"It means run."

She nodded. "I think this also. While they held me, there was much—*como se dice?*—bickering. Many of the men wanted to leave. They are frightened of you, Fargo."

"Glad to hear it. But their leader, Belloch, wants something I have. I'm not sure how he'll play this, but I think he'll keep a few men with him and keep trying to kill me. We should know more after tomorrow."

Rosario touched his charred eyebrows. "What happened? And your *barba*, your beard, too."

"Ah, they'll grow back."

"At least they did not hurt your handsome face."

"Yeah, that's harder to grow back."

Dub and Nate stepped out to meet them.

"How'd we do, Mr. Fargo?" Dub asked. "Was that a frolic or wasn't it?"

"I'm startin' to like crow," Fargo told them. "To think that I once believed you boys couldn't hit a bull in the butt with a banjo. I'm mighty glad I brought you two along."

"So am I," Rosario said, kissing both of them. "All three of you are my heroes."

Fargo handed the boys the shell belts. "When we get back to our camp, pop the cartridges out of their loops and put them in your saddlebags along with the extra handguns."

They crossed the creek to the far side of the tree cover and walked back to the camp, the boys sneaking appreciative glances at the shapely woman.

"Do you like what you see?" she teased them at one point.

"Of course we do," Dub managed. "We didn't mean to stare though, ma'am."

"Rosario. And you may look all you'd like, it is flattering to me. Men *should* look at women. But be more—how do you say, Fargo?"

"Discreet."

She nodded. "Yes, discreet. You are still too young for me— you do not even need to shave yet. But, you are truly real men. If you were older, I would take each of you into the bushes and teach you the secrets of love."

Fargo had to compress his lips hard to keep from laughing

when both boys appeared struck by lightning. Her bold remark silenced both of them for the rest of the walk back.

"What happens next, Mr. Fargo?" Dub said.

"I hate to say it, but that's up to our enemies. From what I know of these border ruffians, today should be the last straw. We've killed and wounded plenty of them, and the main gather will probably dust their hocks east. But not Belloch."

"That pouch, right?"

"What pouch?" Rosario asked.

Fargo quickly explained.

"But if he has failed this long to get it," she asked, "how will he succeed with most of his men gone?"

"That's a poser," Fargo agreed. "He's still the big bug, and chances are he'll keep a few of his best men around him. Or maybe he'll hire more killers in Sublette—the place is lousy with them."

"What about Rosario?" Dub asked. He and his brother were following her advice and sneaking quick glances at her rather than staring. "She can't go back to Sublette now."

Fargo suppressed a grin. "Well, fellows, I was hoping you'd let her sleep here tonight—if you don't mind?"

"*Hell* no," Nate said. "I mean . . . why, she has to sleep some-wheres."

Rosario met Fargo's eye and winked. "But, of course, I will need to bathe in the creek. You boys will guard me?"

"With our lives," Dub assured her.

"And you will not peek? Gentlemen would not."

"Well . . ." The boys looked at each other helplessly, and Fargo burst out laughing.

"I believe you've got these two jays all flummoxed, Rosario. You best skip that bath. If they do peek, and any man would, I'll never get their minds back on this mission. And believe you me, this fight is far from over."

All afternoon Rafe stayed inside his dugout, drinking heavily and listening to the sounds as his decimated band of paid b'hoys rode off in groups of two and three. Each man had been paid a bonus to defuse any possible murder attempt on Belloch. Just in case, however, he kept his dagger in front of him on the deal table. Since killing Jake Ketchum with it, his deadly reputation was known to all, and no man wanted to be the first to come through that entrance with hostile intent.

"Skye Fargo," Rafe said aloud. One man, assisted by two dirt-scratching brats who didn't know poker from faro, had not only destroyed his thirty-man army, he was on the verge of either killing Rafe or sending him to the gallows with the contents of that pouch.

But Rafe had been in tight scrapes before this, and there could be no backing and filling now. Fargo had to die.

"Mr. Belloch?" Moss Harper called from outside, fully aware of that dagger. Rafe smiled.

"Come."

Moss pushed aside the blanket that served as a door, accompanied by two hard-bitten men.

"How'd it go?" Rafe asked him.

"Well, they're all corned up and it was touch and go at first. Some of the men was all wrathy, sayin' they got the little end of the horn just so's the rich toffs in the codfish aristocracy back east could get even richer."

Belloch knew that was in fact the case, and why not? He saw no reason why filthy ruffians who couldn't even quote literature should matter a jackstraw. They were cannon fodder, part of the steaming dung heap.

"Anyhow," Moss resumed, "I reminded 'em how Shanghai was our ramrod, yet he got his brains sprayed all over the place. Then I told 'em how you was gonna lay down a trail for Fargo and draw him off them. That changed their tune in a hurry. And when I gave them all their bonus, *that* put paid to it. They even drunk a toast to you."

"Brilliant work, Moss." Rafe shifted his glance to the other two men. "I recognize these men, of course, but I haven't had the pleasure of meeting them."

"You said to pick our two best men, so that's what I done. This hombre totin' the scattergun is Jed Bledsoe. Jed likes to pack his own shotgun shells. Jed, show Mr. Belloch one of your shells."

Bledsoe cracked open the breech of his Greener 12-gauge, pulled a shell from one of the barrels, and handed it to Rafe.

"It's heavy," Rafe remarked, hefting it. "And isn't that a silver coin I see peeking out at the top?"

"It's packed with Spanish *pesetas*," Bledsoe affirmed. "I double the powder load to make up for the weight. It'll kill five men with one blast if they're close together."

"I seen him cut a tax collector in half with this gun," Moss said. "Just a glancing blow will tear a man's arm clean off."

"I got a dozen more shells like this," Bledsoe added.

Rafe nodded. "Very innovative, Jed. And who's this other gentleman with the beaver hat and the unusual-looking rifle?"

"This here is Levi Carruthers, Mr. Belloch. He was a tracker and scout for the army until he killed an officer for slapping him. He's an expert at hiding in places where there don't seem to be no hiding spots."

"Where we're going, that could be quite useful," Rafe said. "And the rifle?"

"It's a North and Savage revolving percussion rifle," Carruthers explained. "The cylinder is modified to hold twelve cartridges, and when it's empty I can pop the spare cylinder into the breech in about five seconds."

Rafe looked pleased. "Twenty-four shots quick as you want them. Moss, you did well. We can't flush Fargo out, and it's futile to take him on here—he'll just wait us out. Running is now our best option. Our only option. We'll draw him out—onto the open plains. We need to get him into the range of you and your Big Fifty."

"We shoulda fixed his flint when we first spotted him," Moss said. "And them two pups with him can shoot like Texas Rangers."

"You're absolutely right, but that's smoke behind us now. I tell you, given your skill with that Sharps, if we can draw those three out onto the open plains, we can pick them off like lice from a blanket."

Rafe studied the shotgun shell before handing it back to Jed Bledsoe. "We know Fargo is cunning, and he might get in close to us. If that happens we've got Levi's high-capacity rifle, and if it comes down to close combat, Jed's man-slicing scattergun."

"And four sticks of dynamite left," Moss reminded him.

"Exactly. Boys, we have only one objective, and we'll live

and breathe only to achieve it: We need Skye Fargo cold as a wagon tire."

Fargo was up at sunrise and sipping cold coffee as he studied the plains surrounding him. He kicked the boys awake, but let Rosario sleep under an extra blanket taken off one of the outlaws' horses.

"We riding into their camp?" Dub asked, knuckling sleep from his eyes.

"First we're going to circle around it," Fargo said, "and check for sign. I'd wager we'll find out they've lit out for good."

"Maybe Belloch stayed behind," Nate suggested. "You said he needs that pouch."

"Oh, he does. And it would be sweet if we could beard the lion in his den, but that's not likely. These 'agents' made their names by using wit and wile—he'll have a plan. After all, he thinks he's ten inches taller than God, so how can he fail?"

Fargo flipped a silver half dime. "Call it, Nate."

"Lady Liberty."

Fargo uncovered the coin. "Lady Liberty it is. Nate, you stay here and guard Rosario. Dub, you ride with me."

Nate grinned like a butcher's dog while Dub's mouth turned down in a scowl. "Shit, piss, and corruption. Best two out of three."

"Watch that talk with a lady in camp. It's settled, lad. I'll need a good sharpshooter with me if those jayhawkers are still around. Rosario's a nice little bit of frippit, but we've got a job to finish."

"Speaking of Rosario," Dub said. "I woke up last night and both your bedrolls was empty."

"We were stargazing," Fargo said cryptically.

"Uh-huh. *She* saw the stars, all right."

"Stow that line of talk and tack your horse."

Gnawing on jerky in the saddle, both men bore east toward the motte of pines. About a mile out, Fargo tugged rein and curved around to the far side of the trees. Staying out of rifle range, he rode back and forth, leaning out of the saddle to read the ground.

"The main gather rode out, all right," he told Dub. "They left in twos or threes, but all headed due east. They're returning to their old stomping grounds."

Dub, eager to prove he had learned his lessons from Fargo,

jumped down to study the prints. "They didn't leave today, did they? Most of the grass has sprung back up."

"*There's* a plainsman," Fargo praised him. "They left yesterday."

Fargo resumed riding back and forth until he found more tracks, a smaller group this time.

"Here's four riders," he said. "And the trail bears east-northeast. This will be Belloch and the men left with him."

"Why they headed in a different direction?"

Fargo mulled that. "I'd wager because they knew we'd follow the smaller group. If they'd trailed the rest, Belloch was afraid we wouldn't tackle that many riders on the open plains. And we wouldn't, either."

"So he's luring us out a-purpose?"

"Has to be."

Dub gazed out across the endless plains, open and exposed as far as the eye could see. "Damn, it's almighty big."

"For a fact. But at least they can't rimrock us," Fargo joked.

"Us?" Dub repeated. "I was afraid you'd make me and Nate ride home."

Fargo had indeed considered doing that. By himself he could travel faster, and taking on four men was old hat to him. But if these border ruffians chose to scatter on the plains, the boys wouldn't be safe—and, worse, they might be followed back to their farm, jeopardizing Lorena and Krissy.

"We started this trail together," Fargo said. "Now we'll ride it till the end, if that suits you boys."

"It suits us right down to the ground."

Dub thought a moment, then added, "But they might still have more dynamite."

"Yeah, but we'd be fools to let them get close enough to use it. Still, we have to watch for it. Belloch prob'ly picked his most dangerous men for this ride."

"Includin' that one-eyed bastard Moss with the Big Fifty?"

Fargo gave a single nod. "Especially him."

The two men entered the pinewoods cautiously for a quick look around. Empty cans and bottles lay everywhere, as did several corpses covered with shifting, blue-black blankets of buzzing flies.

"Christ Almighty, they don't even bury their dead," Dub said.

"These cold-blooded owlhoots," Fargo said, "wouldn't bury their own mothers on a cool day. C'mon, we have to hurry. We've got to take care of some business back in Sublette, then dust our hocks across the plains. Our quarry has a head start on us, and we don't want to give them time to spring any traps."

With the jayhawkers cleared out, it was safe for Rosario to return to the trading post. The McCallister boys led their dobbins in, and Fargo went inside to dicker with Enis Hagan, one of the owners. He slapped a half eagle on the wooden counter.

"Will this cover the care and feeding of two plow nags until I come back?" Fargo asked. "They won't require grain—just keep them tethered along the creek so they can drink and graze."

"I'll be cut for a steer before I take money from you, Fargo," Hagan said. "You and those two plucky boys not only saved Rosario's life, you drove those border ruffians out of these parts. I will grain them nags, and give 'em the currycomb, too."

"I appreciate the hell right out of that," Fargo said.

"Enis," Rosario spoke up, "Fargo and the boys are not . . . yet."

"You mean, finished?"

"*Eso, sí.* They are going after the *jefe*, and they must have food for this *jornada*, this journey."

"I'll rustle you up some grub for the trail, Fargo. But you three keep your noses to the wind, hear? I know that a man like you wasn't born in the woods to be scared by an owl. But these are some of the most vicious and cunning outlaws I've ever seen, and I'm convinced they were not of woman born—they come straight from hell."

# 14

By early afternoon the three riders were cantering their mounts across the plains under a blistering-hot sun. For ten minutes every hour they dismounted and walked their horses to rest them.

Usually the trail of the four outlaws was so clear that even the boys could spot it without trouble. Now and then, however, a swath of dead grass or a low, rocky spine forced Fargo to dismount and locate the tracks.

Expecting a trap at anytime, ever mindful of Moss and his Big Fifty, the Trailsman kept sending frequent, cross-shoulder glances to either flank.

Nate tilted his hat back and sleeved sweat off his forehead. "Damn, it's hot enough to peel a fence post—if there was any around. I'm spittin' cotton, Mr. Fargo. Can't I have one swallow from my canteen?"

"Just one," Fargo relented. "This late in summer, who knows when we'll find water next?"

"Yessir. But you got a whole gut bag full tied to your horse."

"Yeah, and three thirsty horses with stomachs five times bigger than ours. If our horses give out, junior, we'll soon be feeding worms. Here . . . ."

Fargo rummaged in a saddle pocket and removed three small stones. He popped one in his mouth and handed one to each of the brothers. "Suck on that. It'll keep your mouth moist."

"I ain't seen nobody yet," Dub said. "How 'bout you, Mr. Fargo?"

He shook his head, eyes slitted against the sun.

"They had a good head start on us," Dub added. "Maybe we ain't moving fast enough."

"In this heat, anything faster could drop our horses," Fargo said. "Besides, like I told you, I think they want us to catch up. Belloch wants that pouch like they want ice water in hell."

"Ask me," Nate carped, "we're just barkin' at a knot. Them sons of bitches could be in the Nebraska Territory by now."

"Nobody asked you, titty baby," Dub snapped.

"Teach your grandmother to suck eggs!" Nate fumed.

Fargo laughed. "Nate, you are a caution to screech owls. That would be your grandmother, too, chowderhead."

"Oh. Yeah. I take it back."

"Mr. Fargo," Dub said, "what makes them border ruffians so all-fired mean and rotten?"

"Hell, you boys were all set to join them when I first met you," Fargo reminded him.

"Yeah, but me and Nate are poor as a hind-tit calf. We was ready to join up on account we was hungry, is all."

"That's how plenty of them get started," Fargo said. "Their crops fail, and they band together for food and protection. At first it's just stealing chickens and melons. Next thing you know, it's raids like the one on Lawrence in 'fifty-six that earned this territory the name Bleeding Kansas. Then you get a paper-collar 'agent' like Belloch in the mix, flush with railroad gold, and there's no room for mercy."

"Was your people poor, Mr. Fargo?" Nate asked.

"Out west, son, if a man wants to tell his story, that's fine. But if he doesn't volunteer it, you *don't* nose his backtrail—savvy that?"

"Yessir."

By now they were walking their horses. Fargo halted his companions and knelt to feel the ground with his fingertips.

"I could be wrong," he muttered, "but it feels like a large group of riders approaching from the Smoky Hill River to our north. And I'd guess their horses aren't shod."

The McCallister boys exchanged a troubled glance.

"There's a big Southern Cheyenne summer camp up that way," Dub said.

Fargo nodded, his deep-tanned face resolute of purpose. "My spyglasses won't help—the sun's burning right at the angle I need. Well, we'll just stay frosty and see what happens."

Fargo's matter-of-fact attitude, however, was for the boys' sake and didn't reflect his grim hunch. Sublette, two hours behind them now, was just a stepping-off place. Between that trading post and Fort Hays, about one hundred and fifty miles northeast on their present course, was neither farm nor sheep camp—just desolate plains that were crossed by at least six major Indian tribes, several at war with white men.

"Water your horses from your hats," Fargo ordered before they mounted again.

They rode another half hour or so, Fargo watching the Ovaro's ears. They were the most dependable warning system he'd ever had.

Nate was carrying the provisions in a burlap bag tied to his saddle horn. He pulled out a dried plum and popped it into his mouth.

"This grub is better than we had at the camp," he said, still chewing. "But I'd give a purty for some o' Ma's batter cakes and molasses."

The Ovaro's ears pricked forward, and Fargo knew the three of them were up against it.

"Nate," he said casually, "you're worrying about fleas while tigers eat us alive."

"Huh?"

"Look to the northwest."

"Big group of riders comin' in like all possessed," Dub reported. "But who are they? Jayhawkers?"

"Worse. Southern Cheyennes," Fargo said.

"How can you tell in that bright sun?"

"They're one of the few tribes that ride in formation. The Cavalry calls that a flying 'V.' The brave at the point is their war leader."

"Christ Jesus," Nate said. "Shouldn't we run. They're still a ways off."

"My stallion could probably lose them," Fargo said. "But you two wouldn't stand a snowball's chance."

"These horses we got are at least seventeen hands tall," Dub pointed out. "Pa told us most Indian ponies are about fourteen hands."

"Yeah, but did he also tell you that Plains Indians slit their horses' nostrils so they get more air? They can run full bore upwards of an hour."

"We just gonna sit here?" Nate demanded, his voice wire-tight with nervousness.

"Actually, yes," Fargo said calmly. "Just nerve up, both of you, and listen to me close. Most white men get killed because they don't know how to act around Indians. A Cheyenne warrior despises any man who shows his emotions in his face, especially fear, you take my drift?"

"Yessir," they replied as one.

"Show nothing. No friendliness, no anger, and for Christ sakes, no fear. Don't kowtow, either. It's better to insult a Plains Indian than to lick his moccasins—that shows weakness and fear. They won't likely touch you unless they mean to kill you, but if they speak English they'll maybe try to insult you to test your face. Stuff like how your mother likes to rut with Cheyennes. If that happens, hold your face blank and spit on the ground—but not on them."

The three white men watched the braves approach until they were close enough to make out their eagle-bone breastplates and quill-decorated rawhide leggings.

"Hell, Mr. Fargo," Dub said, "I seen Cheyenne braves before at our place, and they all had long hair. These have cut their hair all ragged and short."

"They've cut it off to mourn their dead," Fargo said. "Most red men take great pride in their hair, so it's a serious sacrifice when they cut it."

Seeing the whites waiting so calmly for them seemed to confuse the Cheyennes. The leader raised one arm, and they walked their mounts slowly closer. Each brave wore a leather band around his left wrist to protect it from the slap of his bowstring. Copper brassards encircled their upper arms.

"Show nothing," Fargo reminded the brothers in a low mutter.

The braves, about a dozen strong, halted ten feet from Fargo's horse. The war leader, whose coup stick was crowded with eagle feathers, watched all three of them from calm and fathomless eyes. His face was blank as windswept stone. Then he stared only at Fargo, and each man gave the other a size-up.

"Tribute," the leader said, pointing first at the Henry in Fargo's saddle scabbard, then the Spencer in Dub's.

Fargo shook his head. "I do not pay tribute. Only cowards do that. No man is my master."

Still expressionless, the leader translated this for his braves. Clearly startled, despite their stone-carved visages, they turned this unexpected reply over carefully in their minds to examine all of its facets.

"You speak strong-heart talk," the leader said. "But you cross our land and must pay tribute."

"The land does not belong to men. Men belong to the land."

Fargo knew that all Indians believed this from the core of their being. The brave translated Fargo's words for the rest, and a few of them reluctantly nodded at the wisdom of his words. Clearly this was an unusual white skin.

"I am Plenty Coups," the Cheyenne said. "How are you called?"

"Skye Fargo."

Plenty Coups nodded. "The Trailsman. For six years I study at the school on the large reservation south of here. I learn to read and write your language. Sometimes I hear of a mah-ish-ta-shee-da, a white man, who speaks one way always. Not from both sides of the mouth, as most white men do."

Despite the praise, Fargo knew that most Indians hated a race traitor and that this remark was a test of his courage.

"All men lie," he replied. "Red men sign treaties just to receive the presents, then break their promises."

Plenty Coups shrugged as if to say he could not deny the ways of men. "White men use Indian skulls to prop open the doors of their lodges."

"I have seen such things. And I have seen Indian parfleches made from the skin of white women and children."

Plenty Coups waved this off as if it were a trifle. Fargo sensed his braves were growing impatient at all this talk, and the war leader feared losing face in front of them.

"You white skins speak of the talking papers called treaties. You speak of how we break our promise. You demand that we live on the worthless land you do not want, then chase us off when the glittering yellow rocks are found there. You demand that we believe in a virgin who had a baby when every man knows this is impossible."

Fargo spat on the ground to show his defiance. "Do I demand that you grow gardens and wear shoes? Or pray to the white man's God? No. I swear by the four directions that, like you, I live beyond the white man's law-ways. Like the red man, I want only to be free."

"Free? Fargo, we did not send out the first soldier—we only sent out the second. Before you mah-ish-ta-shee-da came upon us like locusts, there were always two fires burning in my lodge. One for food, one for friendship. Now this place hears me when I say it, the friendship fire is no more. The white man kills us as surely as he kills the buffalo—for sport. You will pay tribute or we will kill you."

Again Fargo spat defiantly. "Maybe so better not."

"Jesus, you best do it, Mr. Fargo," Nate muttered.

Fargo, hating to do it, backhanded the boy hard, almost knocking him out of the saddle. "Go ask your mother for a dug, whelp. We are in council."

Several Indians nodded, approving of this stern discipline. Fargo looked at Plenty Coups again.

"I have ears for your words," he said. "I do not defend the white men, but the red men have evil ways also. I have watched your tribe run hundreds of buffalo over a cliff, killing them all only to eat one or two. I have seen red men burn the prairie grass as far as the eye can see. And why? Because they are too lazy to put herd guards on their horses. No man, white or red, lives as the High Holy Ones wish us to."

Plenty Coups digested all this, then turned to his companions and conferred in the Cheyenne tongue for several minutes. Then he turned back to Fargo.

"Trailsman, why are you here?"

"I am chasing white killers. They work to build a road for the iron horse. Before your sister, the sun, is born again in the east," Fargo promised, "we will be far from this place."

Plenty Coups nodded. He pointed his streamered lance at an older brave wearing buffalo horns. "This is Eagle on His Journey. Earlier, he threw the bones. You understand?"

Fargo nodded. Plenty Coups meant the pointing bones, ritually tossed inside a magic circle to seek advice from the All-Knowing Ones.

"The bones told our shaman that, this day, we would meet a man whose medicine is powerful. We will not require tribute from you."

"*Ipewa,*" Fargo said in Cheyenne. "Good."

"But will you leave a gift to the place?"

Fargo knew the Cheyenne tribe placed great value on saving

face. This was a euphemism for a face-saving compromise for both sides: the white men could keep their rifles, but must offer something else. He also knew it was not the Indian way to haggle and dicker like white men. A man simply stated his best offer first, and the Indians either accepted or rejected it—perhaps killing you if it was rejected.

Fargo groped in his possibles bag and removed a small magnifying glass, hoping Plenty Coups had never seen one at the school.

He hadn't. Like the other braves he crowded in close, amazed when Fargo showed how it enlarged the pores of Plenty Coups' arm.

"This is a fine toy," Plenty Coups admitted. "Our children will like it. But what use has it for men?"

"It is no toy," Fargo assured him. "It can steal fire from the sun. Watch."

Fargo slid an arrow from the leader's fox-skin quiver and concentrated the merciless sunlight on the tip of a crow feather. When it began smoking, the stoic faces gave way to open astonishment. When a puff of flame sprang up, the braves spoke excitedly among themselves.

"Eagle on His Journey was right," Plenty Coups told Fargo. "Your medicine is powerful. A glass that steals flame from the sun . . . Fargo, you and your companions are safe. Great Maiyun would punish any Cheyenne who harms a medicine man."

Before Fargo handed the magnifying glass over, he faced all four directions of the wind to bless it. This mark of respect excited more discussion from the braves.

"Holy smoke, Mr. Fargo," Nate said when they had resumed their ride, "you sure do know Indians. They was all horns and rattles when they rode up. I thought sure they was gonna lift our dander."

"I didn't want to wallop you like that, Nate," Fargo apologized. "But I had to save face after a young buck spoke up like you did."

"Yeah, I figured that out. *Damn* but you're strong. My head's still ringing."

"All I know," Dub said, "is that we're dang lucky you had that magnifying glass."

"Oh, it wasn't luck," Fargo gainsaid. He reached in his possibles bag and removed three more magnifying glasses. "You can get them back in St. Joe for four bits apiece. I've pulled my own bacon out of the fire more than once with these."

"Four bits?" Dub repeated, grinning. "The big medicine man."

The boys laughed so hard and long that Fargo had to join in. But when their mirth wore off, and they pressed relentlessly to the northeast, Fargo recalled an old saying on the wide-open plains: *You never hear the shot that kills you.*

As the sun dipped lower in the west, sharp gusts turned into howling winds that buffeted them. Fargo watched ghostly tines of lightning shoot down from the sky. A dark thunderhead boiled up on the horizon, and giant claps of thunder shook the ground.

Fargo stripped off his shirt.

"Shouldn't we put our slickers on?" Nate asked. "It's gonna rain like the dickens."

"Sure is," Fargo agreed cheerfully. "That means three things. The horses get cooled off, we get a cool bath, and Moss loses his bead. Feel the air cooling off? Let it rain."

"Yeah, but don't we lose their trail?" Dub asked.

"Lad, by now I know they're *leading* us. Our paths will cross soon enough."

Within minutes a saturated cloud opened up overhead. But as Fargo had explained earlier, heat radiated off the flat-stove surface of the plains and evaporated much of the water. Yet, enough reached the ground to pleasantly revive men and horses.

Storms, on the Great Plains, generally blew in quickly and blew past the same way. In less than twenty minutes the dull yellow ball of sun blazed again on their left flank, though low in the sky now. Open plains lay before them again, with little pockets of water vapor still burning off.

"All seems clear," Dub said.

Fargo nodded. Just then, however, the Ovaro laid his ears back. Fargo hauled back on the reins, then raised a hand to halt his companions. He cleared leather and knocked the riding thong off his Colt.

"The hell?" Dub said. "You can see for miles out here, Mr. Fargo, and it's clear."

"Humor me," Fargo said. "My horse ain't the skittish type,

and he's sending out a warning. Bloody business is close at hand. Fill your hands and keep your eyes peeled."

Fargo thumb-cocked his shooter and nudged the Ovaro forward at a slow walk.

"But there ain't nothing here, Mr. Fargo," Nate said. "The grass ain't high enough to hide a snake."

"Cinch your lips," Fargo snapped in a low voice. "This ain't no Sunday stroll."

Fargo had no idea what he was looking for. There were no trees, no coverts, no rocky spines, no swales even—no place where an ambusher could take shelter. The one thing he had forgotten to consider was a covered rifle pit. It was so far from his thoughts, in fact, that Fargo simply gaped in astonishment when a perfect rectangle of prairie sod was suddenly flung back like a cover, and he stared into the twin, unblinking eyes of a sawed-off shotgun.

# 15

Fargo's moment of stunned immobility passed in a blink, and his tenacious will to live instinctively asserted itself. He got off a snap-shot, blowing the ambusher's lower jaw away, then hit him dead-center in the forehead with his second shot. The McCallister boys, who had once discussed with Fargo their potential to be "gunfighters," were so taken aback by the ambush they never even got a shot off.

"Jerusalem!" Nate exclaimed. "You was right, Mr. Fargo. He's dead, ain't he?"

Dub snorted. "Nate, you turnip head. Look at him—he's dead as a can of corned beef."

The man had toppled over onto one side of the pit. A red rope of blood fountained from his forehead. Fargo dismounted and threw the reins forward, then walked up for a closer look.

"It's a jayhawker, all right. And a pretty ingenious trap. My stallion saved all three of us, boys."

Fargo pried the scattergun from the dead man's grip and broke open the breech. He pulled a shell out, then whistled sharply.

"Great jumping Judas! No wonder this son of a bitch was confident he'd kill all three of us. The shells are packed with *pesetas*, Spanish coins. I've seen one of these shells blow a hole the size of a door in a saloon wall."

Trying to avoid the copious flow of blood, Fargo found a double handful of the special shells in the dead man's ammo pouch. He walked back to Nate's horse.

"Well, I was hoping to get a third good rifle, but this little crowd leveler is even better."

They were already overburdened with weapons, so Fargo pulled the trade rifle from Nate's saddle and tossed it on the ground, replacing it with the scattergun.

"That Indian rifle ain't worth a whorehouse token," he said. "Even the Cheyennes didn't want it."

"That makes three enemies left," Dub said as Fargo turned the stirrup and forked leather. "And one of 'em, at least, knows how to kill on the plains."

"Be dark soon," Nate remarked as they rode out. "We riding all night?"

Fargo shook his head. "Bad idea. In the dark, that ambusher could've cut all three of us down. They don't want to shake us, remember, so no need for a reckless hurry. Besides, the horses need a good rest."

About two miles ahead they encountered a claybank horse, lying on its side and hobbled so it couldn't rise from the grass.

"I wondered where that jasper's horse was," Fargo said, swinging down and stripping all the leather from the mount. He cut the rawhide hobbles and the claybank twisted to its feet, shaking off the saddle and racing across the plains.

"With luck he'll join a wild herd," Fargo said. "If not, he'll die. A horse is like an Indian—he's nothing without the group."

At the time known as "between dog and wolf"—neither day nor night—Fargo called a halt. They stripped their horses of tack, rubbed them dry, and spread the sweat-soaked saddle pads and blankets to dry in the grass. After watering the horses, they placed them on long tethers to graze.

"We better grain them later," Fargo said. "Grass is getting dry."

He opened a can of beans with his knife and shared them with the brothers, eating them cold.

"We'll take turns on guard," he said. "I want both you boys to watch my stallion close. If he starts to toss his head, and especially if he whickers, give the hail."

"You think they know where we are?" Nate asked.

"I'd hate to gamble wrong on that one," Fargo replied. "I didn't spot them, even with spyglasses, and it's not likely they can see us. But it would be easy to follow their backtrail right to us. Stay awake on guard and sleep with your weapons."

Fargo volunteered for the final stint of guard. While the moon clawed higher toward its zenith, he slept fitfully, exhausted but worried about his inexperienced companions. As marksmen they had few peers, and he knew they had plenty of courage, but they were farmers, not frontiersmen.

However, the night passed without incident, and Fargo shook the McCallister boys awake at the first flush of dawn on the horizon.

"It's almost daylight and they know we're dogging them," Fargo said, "so I'm boiling a handful of coffee beans. We'll eat in the saddle. Tend to your weapons, then your horses. And don't forget to inspect their feet."

Each man drank two cups of coffee so strong it made the boys shudder.

"Lissenup," Fargo said. "Our quarry may no longer be ahead of us. They could be on our flanks, or even behind us, setting Moss up with that Big Fifty. Once we hit leather, we raise our skyline considerably. A Sharps, in the hands of a prone shooter, can drop a horse at fifteen hundred yards, a man at a thousand. So today we ride in single file, and keep fifty feet between each of us."

He looked at Nate. "I'll ride first and watch what's ahead of us. You take the middle and watch both flanks. Dub, I want you to ride drag and get a sore neck watching our backtrail."

They both nodded. "Think there'll be trouble today, Mr. Fargo?" Dub asked.

"I'd bet my horse on it. Belloch hasn't got the manpower to openly stop me from going to a fort, and he wants that pouch the way the devil wants souls."

"If Belloch really killed that senator," Nate said, "shouldn't he be took prisoner steada killed like the rest?"

"Personally," Fargo said, "I'd like to decorate a cottonwood with him, or even drag-hang him behind my horse. But we won't kill him unless we have to. I ain't crying in my beer for any politician, but General Hoffman was a good soldier and popular with the troops, and the army deserves a crack at Belloch."

"Won't the government back in Washington City want him?"

"Believe me, boy, the army knows how powerful the railroad lawyers are, and they won't send him back. Besides, Territorial law applies out here first, not U.S., so he'll spend some time in the crowbar hotel at a fort, then be fitted for a hemp necktie. First, though, the army will want to know what's going on with these railroad wars."

Fargo whistled in the Ovaro and inspected his tack: saddle, cinches, latigos, stirrups, bridle, and reins. Then he rigged his horse and inspected each of the stallion's hooves, prying out a few small stones.

"Let's make tracks," he called out. "And remember: one man daydreaming, out here, could get all of us killed."

After a long search, Rafe Belloch lowered his field glasses and turned to his two companions.

"It's hopeless by now, gents. Bledsoe was supposed to kill them, then run ahead for his horse and ride all night to meet us. It's past four p.m., and not a speck on the horizon."

"No sign of Fargo's bunch either?" Moss Harper asked.

"No. But I'd guess they camped last night."

Levi Carruthers, busy rolling a quirly, shook his head in bafflement. "I can't figure it, Mr. Belloch. I can't cipher nor write, like you, but I know the science of killing. That was a perfect trap."

"It was clever," Belloch agreed. "I suspect the weak link was Bledsoe. Men like Fargo develop the reflexes of a cat. Bledsoe must have taken a moment too long to fling the sod aside and get his shot off."

"You said there's no sign of Fargo, either," Moss interjected. "What if we lost him?"

Belloch shook his head. "They say Fargo could follow a wood tick across solid rock. Besides . . ." He pointed at the buffalo-chip fire burning nearby. They had built it in a pit because of powerful wind gusts that had been building for hours. "He can't miss that smoke."

"If you're right, Mr. Belloch," Levi said, "that means Fargo has Jed's scattergun and all them coin-loaded shells. That gun could take the vinegar out of a she-grizz protectin' her cubs."

"Not if we snuff their wicks first," Moss said. "And we will."

"Bravo, Moss," Rafe said. "You just placed the ax on the helve. That's the confidence that Shanghai lacked. We're fools if we wait for Fargo to close with us. We'll seize the initiative while he's out in the open, vulnerable."

Levi Carruthers, who had spent more time on the frontier than either of these men and knew about Fargo, took an ember from the fire and lit his cigarette, saying nothing. But he was worried about Belloch's sanity. Despite all that Fargo had inflicted on them in just over a week, Belloch still acted like a man who held the high ground and all the escape trails.

Rafe noticed his silence. He had to raise his voice above the gusting wind. "Levi, you seem skeptical."

"Well, what I've seen and heard of Fargo? He's no man to rate low. That trap we put Jed in—that's never come a cropper before this."

"Oh, Fargo's a top hand, for a fact, and killing him will not be a featherbed job. But we'll get it done. Granted, he's all grit and a yard wide, but he hasn't got the mentality to match wits with me . . . us, I mean."

Rafe's horse, a light tan palomino with ivory mane and tail, fought against its picket, skittish from the increasing wind.

"Quite a blow making up," Moss remarked. "And we're headed right into it."

Levi nodded, trying to protect his cigarette. "This'll be an all-nighter. Might be best to camp right here and double-tether the horses."

"Maybe," Rafe said, glancing around. "But we'll have to use up valuable grain on the horses. I noticed it miles back—the grass is high and it's not quite dead, but it's brown and dry. These central plains have seen little rain."

"Jesus, Moss," Levi said. "Mr. Belloch just hit on it."

"Hit on what?"

Levi's weather-beaten face creased in a grin. "'Member how we done for them pukes at Hutchinson? The ones camped in that draw?"

Moss snapped his fingers. "Oh, yeah! This now is even better."

Belloch followed all this with avid interest. "I'm open to new plans, gents, but it helps if I know what they are."

Moss grinned. "Sure, boss. Try this on for size . . ."

Late in the afternoon Fargo called a halt to water the horses.

"Looks like I might win your horse," Dub roweled him, speaking close to Fargo's ear to be heard above the wind. "You bet your horse we'd be attacked somehow today."

"I've got until midnight," Fargo reminded him. "Bet's still on."

The wind quieted for a few moments, calming the horses.

"I'm glad the sons of bitches are leaving us alone," Nate said. "Proves we got 'em scared."

"Not a smart way to think," Fargo gainsaid. "When you can't see your enemy is when you start worrying."

Nate, who looked weary from his eyes to his insteps, loosed a frustrated sigh. "Even if we got 'em scared they're halfway to Canada by now—why dog them if we run 'em off for good?"

"I know it's hard slogging, Nate. But trouble never goes away on its own if you run away from it. Besides, their fresh trail means they're closer than you think. And this Belloch has to be treated like a distempered wolf—you don't run him off, you kill or capture him. C'mon, we're burning daylight."

They hit leather and gigged their horses forward, the wind kicking back up and billowing dust around them. They tied their neckerchiefs over their mouths and noses, tugging their hats down to protect their eyes.

"Why so damn much dust?" Dub complained. "There's plenty of tall grass."

"Yeah, but it's dry and on the featheredge of dying," Fargo said. "That means the roots are weak and can't hold the dry soil in place. Hell, you're a farmer—you should know that."

Fargo did his best to stay alert for the ever-expected attack, but conditions were deteriorating rapidly. The terrible shrieking of the wind rubbed his nerves raw, and though the trail-seasoned Ovaro was standing up to it well, the outlaws' horses were fighting the reins.

When the next gust abated for a moment, Fargo shouted, "No use, boys. Your horses will bolt if we keep it up. Throw their bridles, then turn them downwind and hobble picket them. Kick the picket pins in extra deep. When your mounts settle down, strip them down to the neck leather and rub them down good."

The three men sat with their backs to the wind and shared a hunk of salt pork that Enis Hagan had included with their provisions. Fargo watched the sun, hazed to a dull copper by the billowing dust, sink below the western horizon.

"This wind will keep up until late," he predicted. "We might's well turn in. Who wants first watch?"

"I'll take it," Nate shouted above the pandemonium of the wind. "Who could sleep in all this consarn racket?"

"All right, but don't assume we're safe just because there's a howler blowing. This is a perfect time for an enemy to sneak up on us. Dub, I'll take the second trick and let you sleep longer."

Fargo lay his Henry, Colt, and knife ready to hand and rolled into his blanket, head resting in the bow of his saddle. This was his ninth day of little rest, bad rations, and constant danger. With the wind shrieking like a soul in torment, he closed his weary eyes and massaged them with his thumbs. Then he pulled his hat down over the top of his face, falling into an uneasy sleep.

Enis Hagan's words chased him down a long tunnel into the Land of Nod: *I know that a man like you wasn't born in the woods to be scared by an owl. But these are some of the most vicious and cunning outlaws I've ever seen, and I'm convinced they were not of woman born—they come straight from hell.*

# 16

Fargo's dream was turning quickly into a nightmare.

Years earlier, in the New Mexico Territory, he had launched a desperate manhunt for one of the sickest, most cunning murderers he had ever faced: arsonist "Blaze" Weston, who reveled in burning young girls to death in their beds, setting entire towns on fire, and searing pristine landscapes for the sheer, perverse feeling of power.

Once he had trapped Fargo in a burning circle of death, and only the Ovaro's ability to leap over it had saved man and horse. Now, as he tossed fitfully in his sleep, Fargo again heard the roaring crackle of hungry flames, felt the blistering heat growing more intense, smelled the acrid stench of dry grass being consumed . . .

The high-pitched whinny of a frenzied horse brought Fargo back to the here and now. He sat up and felt his blood seem to stop and flow backward in his veins.

The night sky was lit up in a lurid yellow-orange, and due north of the campsite, a wind-whipped wall of fire raced straight at him.

Nate, relieved earlier by his brother on guard, was snoring in his blanket. And Dub, who should have been awake and alert, sat sound asleep with his head slumping onto his chest.

"Jesus Christ," Fargo swore, his limbs filled with an icy panic he knew he must master. That fire, stretching toward both flanks as far as the eye could see, was greatly accelerated by a tornadic wind, and time was of the essence.

Fargo sprang to his feet, drew his Colt, and fired it. The sound brought both McCallister boys instantly awake.

"Moses on the mountain!" Dub exclaimed.

"Shut up and listen!" Fargo shouted above the roar of wind

and fire and the panicked screaming of the horses. "We're all going to die hard unless you follow my orders. Strip off your shirts and tie them over your horse's eyes. If they can't see the fire, they'll calm down some."

This order was easier to give than to execute, but luckily the horses were hobbled, and soon all three mounts were blindfolded. Their panic degraded to extreme nervousness.

"We can't outrun this fire because the horses won't run blindfolded," Fargo said, "and they'll go wild if we uncover their eyes. So throw your saddles on, gather all your weapons, and stand by."

The wall of fire rushed at them like a living, malevolent force. Fear throbbed in Fargo's palms, but he refused to let it rattle him.

Fortunately Fargo had replenished his supply of lucifers at the trading post. He rummaged in a saddle pocket until he found his can of gun oil, then snatched up his blanket from the ground and soaked one corner of it with the oil.

"God Almighty, Mr. Fargo!" Nate cried out. "We're gonna burn alive!"

"Nerve up and *shut* up!" Fargo snapped. "If it comes down to certain death by fire, remember you've got guns to take the fast way out. But hold off on that—we ain't licked yet."

The first match Fargo thumb-scratched to life instantly blew out in the fierce wind. Cursing, crouching to protect the next one with his body, he finally set the blanket ablaze. Moving exactly parallel with the rolling comber of approaching fire, Fargo dragged the blanket in a long line, setting a backfire.

There was only one chance: to burn enough of the grass before the main fire reached them, robbing it of fuel and allowing the men and horses to seek refuge in the burned area. But even though the dry grass burned quickly, the ground was hot with embers and a horse's hoof is sensitive to heat. Would it cool enough in time to lure the horses into the burned-out swath?

"Mr. Fargo!" Dub shouted. "It's on us!"

Fargo could feel the moisture on his eyes drying up, and wind-driven embers were singeing his buckskins.

"Untie their hobbles and cut the pickets!" Fargo shouted. "Drive them forward any way you have to!"

What happened next astounded all three men. The two geldings rebelled as soon as their front hooves hit the hot ground, rearing up and knocking both boys aside. But Fargo's dominant stallion, with the spirit and fight of an uncut horse, drove both geldings forward by biting on their necks. It was for moments like this, Fargo marveled, that he refused to geld a horse.

"Get as far forward as you can stand it, boys," Fargo ordered, feeling the heat through his soles. "And get your guns ready in case this doesn't work. Shoot your horse first, and then eat your muzzle. But wait for my order."

For several excruciating minutes the issue remained in doubt. Acrid, billowing smoke made it almost impossible to breathe, but the roaring wind gusts helped by whisking it away. The wall of fire, perhaps as tall as Fargo, edged right up to them and blasted them with furnace heat.

Fargo feared he had finally reached the end of his last trail. Then, almost instantly, the line of fire nearest them simply died out. It raged on both sides and behind them, but the little burned-out island Fargo had created was just enough to save them.

When the ground cooled enough, the three men hobbled the horses and sat down, watching in silent fascination as the fire devoured the plains behind them.

"Belloch's bunch did that, didn't they?" Nate said, his voice bitter.

"Who else? There was no lightning."

"You gave them Indians a magnifying glass," Dub reminded him. "Maybe they was playing with it."

"They're well behind us, and this fire came from the north. It's Belloch's bunch, all right. Christ knows how much of the plains they've burned."

In another hour dawn broke in a salmon pink streak on the eastern horizon. Shortly after, the full extent of the destruction was graphically clear. As far as the eye could see the plains were charred black, and wraiths of smoke still hovered. Red-tailed hawks and other birds that normally sought mice and other prey circled in confusion, while vultures swooped low everywhere, feasting on animals that didn't beat the flames.

"It's ugly now," Fargo said, "but not all that serious. Lightning does this all the time. That grass was dying anyway, and there'll be new growth next spring."

"You saved our lives, Mr. Fargo," Dub said, extending a hand.
Instead of shaking it, Fargo doubled his fist and caught Dub

with a cowcatcher that lifted the boy off his feet and sent him sprawling on the charred ground.

"Listen to me, both of you," Fargo said. "This fire wasn't your fault. But if either one of you little shits falls asleep on guard duty again, I'll kill you for cause. We're at war right now, and in wartime there's no greater crime than sleeping on guard. I *won't* tolerate it. Do I make myself clear?"

"Yessir," they both replied, Dub massaging the point of his chin. Fargo reached out a hand to help him up.

"Criminy, Mr. Fargo," he said, "I'm really sor—"

"Whack the cork, Dub. I know you're sorry, and I know you won't do it again. By the way, both you boys did a good job last night following orders. Since there's smoke all over anyway, I'm gonna whip us up a breakfast of sourdough biscuits and bacon— we sure's hell earned it."

Belloch stared through his field glasses, anger mixed with incredulity. "Look at Fargo. Daniel emerging from the den of lions. Or better yet: Shadrach from the furnace. And those two seed-stickers with him. Not to mention all three horses. Fargo is definitely our hair shirt, gents."

"God-*damn* it!" Moss Harper exploded. "Boss, I never heard of no fellow named Shadrach, but I swear to you that me and Levi set a rip-roarin' fire. All three of them crusaders should be charred meat by now."

"Oh, I don't fault you two, Moss," Belloch said, lowering his glasses. "I can see it was a hell of a fire—you've turned the prairie black. But somehow, some way, Fargo got them through it."

Belloch's suit looked baggy and dusty, and the boiled shirt was stained from dirt and sweat. But his confident, determined manner had not lowered a notch. Adversity always brought out his fighting spirit, and the tougher his opponent, the more he enjoyed the contest.

"Well," he said, "our pitfall trap didn't work, and neither did a grass fire. We have four sticks of dynamite, but absolutely no chance to get close enough, in these wide-open plains, to use it. So it looks like we're down to our hole card. They say there's only one god in the West, and his name is Sam Colt. Bullets are our only chance now, boys, and that brings it down to Moss."

Moss raised his Big Fifty. "Well, Sam Colt didn't make this blazin' firestick, but it'll kiss the mistress, all right."

"Hold on," Levi Carruthers said. "You're wrong about the dynamite, boss. We can send Fargo up the flume with it."

"How so?"

"Before sundown I scouted ahead a few miles. The Pawnee River is straight ahead of us about an hour's ride. It's dried to jerky, but a hundred yards past it there's a waterhole fed by an underground spring."

"All right," Belloch said. "Crack the nut and expose the meat. How does that get us close enough to use dynamite? We have neither detonating cord nor plungers, just thirty-second fuses."

Levi flashed his toothless smile. "We won't need them. In fact, we're gonna shorten the fuses because we have something just as good as a plunger on the open plains—we have a big, leafy tree."

Just before midmorning the burned-out grass abruptly ceased in a line almost as straight as a knife edge.

"Here's where they started the fire," Fargo said, taking out his field glasses. "Now we'll have to pick up their trail again. It'll be somewhere close by. Boys, light down. No use skylining ourselves while we're not riding."

Fargo swung his right leg over the cantle and dismounted, then tossed the reins forward. He studied the plains before them with studious care.

"Nothing," he announced. "Just brown grass and blue sky as far as I can see."

"That's all there is out here," Nate complained. "The big empty. You know, Mr. Fargo, me and Dub ain't never even seen a mountain in our lives. Just some hills. Bet you seen 'em all, huh?"

"Oh, I've missed a few small ranges in the Northwest and Mexico, but otherwise, if they're in the West, I've seen 'em. But the finest ranges you could ever visit are the Canadian Rockies."

Fargo, leading the Ovaro, was walking the fire line now, looking for his quarry's trail.

"Don't make no never mind to me," Nate said. "Any mountain will do."

"Well, don't wait too long," Fargo advised. "The West is going to hell on a fast horse. Hydraulic miners are already washing the mountain slopes away. Twenty years, at most, and the frontier will mostly be fences, roads, and the rattle and hullabaloo of cities from El Paso to the Bitterroot Range. Manufactories, mines, railroads, sawmills . . . and drifters like me will be arrested as vagrants."

"There weren't none of that when you was our age?" Dub asked.

Fargo shook his head, still studying the ground. "I knew the West when the mountain-man era was just ending and there was hardly anybody out here but Indians, a few prospectors, and the last of the fur traders. Oh, there were a few pilgrims up north on the Oregon Trail, but they bothered no one."

"Ma's from Cincinnati," Nate said. "She says big cities are exciting."

"I s'pose they are, for a woman," Fargo agreed. "They have dress shops, milliners, churches, lecture halls—all the things women like, God love 'em. Hell, a woman values a new hat the way a man values a hand-tooled saddle. Me, I've been to plenty of big cities, but I can't abide the filth and the stink and the people crowded in like maggots in cheese."

"I'll take your word on big cities, Mr. Fargo," Dub said. "But I'm hanged if I can see how you sleep on the ground every night. It's got me sore all over. I miss my bed."

Fargo grinned. "I like a bed now and then myself, but soft beds make soft soldiers. Anyhow, before you spread your groundsheet and blanket, just soften up the ground good with your knife. Say . . . here's the trail, boys."

Fargo pointed to flattened grass indicating three riders, still bearing north-northeast. The flat prints told him they were recent.

"It's got me treed," Fargo said. "They're still headed straight toward Fort Hays. Why would Belloch want me drawing closer to soldiers when I've got that pouch?"

"Maybe it ain't what you think," Dub suggested. "You just been guessing it's bad news for Belloch."

"I hate to say it, Dub," Fargo admitted, "but you could be right. But then, why the hell does he want it so bad?"

"Open it," Nate urged. "Then we'll know."

Fargo shook his head. "That military courier was clear in his message to the Quakers—it's to be delivered unopened to a military officer. I'll tell you this much—Belloch has some kind of plan in mind in case we reach that fort. Anyhow, let's stow all this jaw-jacking."

Fargo swung up into leather, the boys following suit. "We rolled a seven last night with that fire," he warned them. "Since we left Sublette, they've come close to killing us twice. And they ain't done trying, so keep your mind on what we're doing. This bunch may be gutter filth, but they're experts at helping a man get his life over quick."

# 17

For perhaps another two hours Fargo and his young companions rode on, holding their horses to an easy trot in the searing afternoon heat. Fargo pointed to a meandering line of stunted cottonwoods and juniper trees ahead.

"That's the Pawnee River. Even when its banks are full with snowmelt you can prac'ly spit across it. By now it's dry, but if we dig into the bed we can make a seep pool of clean water and let the horses tank up good."

When they were perhaps a hundred yards out, Fargo halted the brothers. "Break out your rifles boys, then dismount and cover me. That tree line is scraggly, but I don't trust this bunch. Let me scout it first."

Drawing his Colt, Fargo let the Ovaro walk slowly closer, still following the trail. At the dried-up river, Fargo worked his way along the bank in both directions, easily verifying that no one waited in ambush. He waved the boys in.

"They crossed here," he said, pointing to fresh prints in the river bed. "Notice how the edges of the prints still hold their shape in the dirt? That means they can't be more than a few hours ahead of us—a dirt track starts to crumble after that."

Fargo leathered his shooter and pulled a U.S. Army entrenching tool from the loops on his saddle fender. But as he started to dig, a lone cottonwood tree caught his eye about a hundred yards past the far bank of the river.

"That tree's big and in good shape," he told the boys. "Good chance there's a water hole beside it. Lots of times you'll find a good one just back of a river. In case I'm wrong, you two start digging."

Fargo grabbed the coin-loaded scattergun from Nate's saddle boot and set out on foot, still following the trail. Soon he spotted sunshine gold-leafing the surface of a water hole the size of a large cabin. But instead of following the tracks to the water's edge, he circled wide around the water and checked the opposite side.

Sure enough, three horses had ridden to the hole, and three had ridden out.

Still, something about that tree made Fargo's scalp tingle. He studied it closely, its sun-shot leaves fluttering in the breeze, large and leathery.

Fargo spotted no one hiding in it, but from his present angle he couldn't see all the inner branches. He raised the scattergun and moved in on cat feet until he was close to the gnarled bark, then peered up cautiously.

The glaring sunlight of the plains made it difficult to see clearly in the dark maze of leaves. Fargo breathed deeply through his nose, detecting a faint odor like burning rope, but the stiff breeze made it difficult to be sure.

Burning rope . . . often used to light fuses because the glowing rope lasted longer than matches.

Realization jolted through him, and Fargo squeezed both triggers of the scattergun, blowing a tunnel upward through the branches. A man loosed a banshee scream of pain. Next rattle out of the box, a sparking stick of dynamite plunged right toward Fargo's upturned face.

In real time it took perhaps two seconds, but to Skye Fargo it was a terrifying eternity. There was no time to think, only react. His gun hand was filled, so he doubled up his left fist and drove a hard, straight-arm punch straight up, hitting the dynamite squarely.

He leaped sideways, hit the ground in a ball and rolled as fast as he could until a powerful explosion shook the ground and showered him with leaves, splintered wood—and wet, clammy gobbets of human flesh and organs.

Dub's voice: "Mr. Fargo! You alive?"

He could hear both boys racing toward him.

"Still sassy, boys," he called out. "But a little jittery. They damn near sent me over the range that time."

"Good God Almighty!" Nate exclaimed, paling. "Is them guts hanging off your hat?"

"Nate, you dimwit," Dub scoffed. "Does he look like his guts are blowed out?"

"It was the jasper waiting up in the tree," Fargo said, wiping

*143*

his hat off in the grass. "I must've shot him just as he dropped the dynamite. They tricked me by leading his horse out so I thought all three were gone."

"If he dropped the dynamite," Dub said, "how's come the top of the tree is gone?"

Fargo stood up, his legs a little shaky. "I slugged it in midair, sent it sailing right back up to him."

"Between them coin shells and the dynamite, no wonder there's guts all over the place. Look at the water hole."

Fargo did. Leaves and branch fragments were interspersed with human gore.

"Boys," he said, "we won't be drinking from that mess. Let's get back and dig that hole."

"That's three times they've tried to kill us since we left Sublette," Nate said as they walked back to the Pawnee River.

Fargo nodded. "And if Belloch is as smart as I think he is, the last man with him is Moss Harper—Moss, and that widow-maker of his."

"Widow-maker?" Nate repeated. "So what? None of us is married."

Fargo laughed and punched Nate's arm. "*That's* the gait, boy. So what if they kill us long as they don't eat us, right?"

Before they rode out, Fargo and the McCallister boys checked their horses' hooves for cracks and stone bruises.

"Keep your eyes to all sides," Fargo warned them as they hit leather. "And remember how I told you to search open terrain. A Sharps is large caliber with a powder load of seven hundred and fifty grains in the shell. That's three times my Henry and double the Spencer, so range is our weak card. It's single-shot, but it's lever action, and you can count on four or five shots a minute from it."

"This Belloch just keeps coming at us," Dub said.

"He's no halfway man, I'll give him that. The fight's been harder since he drew us out onto the plains."

"I reckon his kind figure they can't lose."

"He'll foul his nest," Fargo said. "They always do."

"All this killin' of innocent people," Nate said, "just for a railroad. It don't make no sense."

"It's not the railroad itself," Fargo said. "It's all the money that surrounds it. Whoever gets that contract for a cross-country line will control this nation."

"Ain't that why we whipped the English?" Dub asked. "So we'd be *free* of control?"

"'Pears to me," Fargo said, "that no man can ever be truly free—it's just a question of how much control and destruction we have to tolerate. I don't mind a little honest law, or a hard-working man making a good living for his family by cutting down a few trees to sell lumber. But right now the money-grubbers in top hats are dividing the West up among themselves, and no law is stopping them from outright theft."

"I believe you, Mr. Fargo," Nate said. "Pa said the same thing. But Ma and Krissy are right—it will be fine to cross the country in a week steada four months."

Fargo sleeved sweat off his forehead, eyes in constant motion. The heat radiating off the baked plains made the air waver and blur.

"Nate, I'll give you that," he replied. "Men have a right to progress. If I didn't have repeating firearms, I'd be dead by now. But if they do run a railroad through here, late-summer heat will warp the rails. That, or the Indians will learn how to use crowbars and pull the rails up like they do back east. Trains might be safe someday, but plenty of pilgrims will die at first. Hell, boilers on steamships blow up all the time, killing hundreds."

The trio rode cautiously north-northeast under a cloudless blue sky as vast as eternity. Every ten minutes or so Fargo swept the horizon with his field glasses.

"See anything?" Dub asked.

"Nah, but heat ripple is bad. I wish I could see 'em. Belloch is pee doodles, but I don't like not knowing where Moss is."

Fargo had barely finished speaking when he felt a sharp tug on the left side of his shirt, followed by the crack of a large-bore rifle. He heard a sickening impact to his right and feared one of the boys had been hit. But it was Nate's horse that collapsed to the ground, blood spuming from its head.

"Swing your legs clear!" Fargo shouted.

"By the Lord Harry!" Dub exclaimed as his brother went sprawling.

"Nate, crawl behind your horse!" Fargo ordered. "Dub, light down and copy me!"

Fargo knew Moss was reloading, and figured they had maybe fifteen seconds at most. He leaped down, grabbed the Ovaro around the neck, and wrestled him down. Dub's sorrel took a few seconds longer, but following the stallion's lead soon lay flat in the grass.

Another shot ranged in, snapping just over their heads.

"He'll get our horses, too, won't he?" Dub asked.

"Maybe, but only if he's lucky. No ground is really flat, even out here, and he's shooting from a prone position. He can't have a clear view of us."

"Where is the son of a bitch?" Nate asked. "Let's fire back."

"Don't be a fool," Fargo said. "Wherever he is, he's way past our range."

A third shot kicked up dirt and grass just in front of them. The Ovaro was bullet savvy, but the sorrel struggled to stand and run. Nate joined his brother in holding the gelding down.

"All right," Fargo said, "let's stay frosty and work out the ballistics. The ball tore through the left side of my shirt, front to back, then tagged Nate's horse, who was behind me and to my right. That puts our shooter northwest of us at about ten o'clock."

The next shot thwacked the dead horse in the rump.

"Now we're whistling," Fargo said, studying the terrain with his spy glasses. "I can see powder smoke over his general position, but not Moss. He's shooting from a shallow draw ahead and on our left."

Fargo slid his Henry from its boot. "Let's face it, boys. Right now we're neither up the well nor down. We've got to make a play—rearguard actions won't save us. You game?"

"Hell," Dub said, "Pa always said it's better to buck out in smoke than get cut down like a dog on the run."

"Wish I could've met that pa of yours," Fargo said. "The West needs more plow pushers like him."

The next slug from the Big Fifty nicked Fargo's saddle fender.

"Here's the play. Dub, bring your Spencer. It's got better range than my Henry. We're gonna run right at the dry-gulching bastard, but not in a straight line, hear? Don't give him an easy bead. I'll show you where to shoot while we're heading in. You've only got seven rounds, so hold and squeeze. I've got sixteen, so as soon as we get in range, I'll pepper the son of a bitch with lead."

"What about me?" Nate asked.

"You get that scattergun out, then you play dead. If Moss kills us, he'll come up here to get that pouch. Soon as he's in range, blow him to stew meat. Then take my horse and deliver that pouch to Fort Hays."

Fargo was pointing out the draw when the next slug hornet buzzed past his ears. "Goddamn it, Dub, I don't like being close-herded like this by lead. Let's give him a taste of his own medicine. Adjust your sights."

Dub raised the sight vane on his carbine while Fargo adjusted the aperture on his Henry a few clicks, sighting out another hundred yards. As soon as the next round whined over, Fargo yelled, "Run!" and both men broke cover to take off at a dead run.

Fargo, estimating reload time, yelled, "Swerve!" Both men changed course abruptly just before the next report of the Big Fifty.

"Okay, Dub!" he shouted. "Shoot into that pocket of dead grass at the end of the draw."

Dub opened fire, loosing three shots.

"Swerve!" Fargo shouted, and again Moss missed.

"Empty that thunder stick!" Fargo shouted, and by the time the Spencer fell silent, Fargo's Henry, the weapon "you load on Sunday and fire all week," was tossing a steady stream of lead into the grass—so steady that Moss got ice in his boots and bolted toward the west end of the draw. By now Fargo was close enough to spot Moss's horse tethered there. He was drawing a bead on it when the one-eyed man gave a mighty toss, and Fargo knew what he had to be throwing.

"Hit the deck!" he screamed at Dub, both men flattening themselves in the grass just before the ground was rocked by an explosion that showered them with dirt and grass.

The dynamite had fallen well short of Fargo and Dub, but the smoky diversion was enough to cover Moss's escape.

"We got the yellow-bellied skunk," Dub said, breathing heavy after their hard run in the heat. "It didn't work, Mr. Fargo, but you had a good plan."

"Oh, it worked fine," Fargo assured him. "I never thought we'd kill him. Moss cost us a horse, but by charging him we made him cut his losses. And after all that lead we threw at him, I'll bet you all the color on the Comstock that coward never ambushes us again."

# 18

Fargo and his companions made a rough camp after dark, sharing dried fruit and another can of beans.

"You boys can't keep riding double," Fargo said, watching the plains under a moon bright enough to make shadows. "The days are getting hotter than the hinges of hell. So every hour, when we dismount and walk the horses, Nate can switch off between me and Dub."

"If you're right," Dub said, "and they're done attacking us, that must mean they're on the prod, right? And how we gonna catch 'em on two horses?"

Fargo cocked his head—he thought he'd heard a rustle in the dry grass, but it might have been the fitful wind.

"Belloch won't take the geographic cure," Fargo predicted. "He'd be a wanted man, and his kind can't survive back of beyond."

"Then what choice has he got?" Nate pressed. "You think he's got a hideout around here?"

"Hideout?" Fargo snorted. "Hell, there's nothing on these plains you could hide a memory in. Not until you get to the sand caves way up north. Remember, Belloch is used to having the whip hand. I think he's got a play in mind, and it involves Fort Hays."

"But if he killed that senator and a general—"

"No 'if,' he did it," Fargo insisted. "Or actually, ordered it done. But sometimes the best way to get out of trouble is to go right *into* it."

Dub said, "Sorta his version of running toward the guns?"

"In a manner of speaking," Fargo agreed.

This time the rustling noise was more distinct and definitely not the wind.

"Fill your hands, boys," he ordered in a low tone, drawing his Colt. "We might have company."

Fargo pulled the hammer to half cock, to avoid the noise that might alert an intruder. He waved the brothers down flat onto the ground.

The rustling grew closer and Fargo, crouched low, suddenly rushed toward it. The boys flinched when a gun barked.

"Mr. Fargo?" Dub called. "You all right?"

"It's over, boys. I killed the dirty snake!"

"Moss?" Dub said eagerly.

"Belloch?" Nate chimed in.

Fargo stepped into view with a four-foot rattlesnake dangling from his left hand. "I didn't have time to catch his name, fellows, but he's invited to supper. Nate, scoop us out a fire pit while I skin this rascal. Tonight we're having fresh meat."

On the twelfth day since Fargo witnessed the savage attack on the Quakers, the outline of Fort Hays, central Kansas Territory, rose into view on the horizon.

"I told you that cunning bastard means to pull a rabbit out of a hat," Fargo said. "We've stayed on Belloch and Moss's trail, and it's headed right for the fort. We're finally gonna get a look-see at this 'agent.'"

"I still can't reason it out," Dub said. "I thought he was a-scairt of that pouch."

"Don't forget," Fargo warned the boys, "there's the story about me dressing up like a border ruffian to strike the Quakers. Sure as cats fighting, Belloch got that lie started."

"But you said you done work for the army for years now. They going to believe that hogwash?"

Fargo shrugged one shoulder. "The army's a contrary and notional creature. Its best people have the least power. All we can do, boys, is take the bit in our teeth and trust to the facts. Matter fact, this ain't none of your picnic. Why not hang back and let me handle this fandango?"

"The hell?" Dub protested. "Ain't we sided you through most of this?"

"With distinction," Fargo admitted.

"'Sides, we're witnesses," Nate added. "We didn't see that

deal with the Quakers, but we seen what these sons of bitches done to Rosario and Cindy."

"Yeah, but remember," Fargo warned, "you can start out as a witness and turn into the accused. If Belloch pulls this off, you two could hang with me."

"Tough titty," Nate said. "I'd consider it a distinction to hang beside a man like you. Alongside my pa, you're the toughest, bravest hombre I ever met. And the most honorable, too."

"I second all that," Dub said.

Fargo, who was not one to slop over, nonetheless felt a lump in his throat. "I ain't got the words, boys. I'll treasure that praise for the rest of my days."

By now the details of the frontier fort were clearly visible. Log walls twelve feet high and loop-holed for rifles, with guard towers at the four corners, surrounded it. Cavalry horses grazed nearby under guard. The wide front gate stood open, and Fargo knew he and his companions were in trouble when an armed detail of about a dozen men rode out to intercept them.

"Just bite your tongues," Fargo said, "and let me handle this."

When the detail was about thirty yards out, the enlisted men brought their carbines to the ready.

"Throw down your arms," called out a young lieutenant barely older than Dub.

Fargo didn't recognize the shavetail, but the sergeant, Jim McGreevey, was an old acquaintance. "Say, Jim, what's all the whoop-dee-do? We were riding in under our own steam."

McGreevey eyed the dusty, rumpled, singed, exhausted-looking trio. "Skye, all three of you look like you been riding the grub line."

"I said throw down your arms!" the lieutenant repeated, for some reason drawing his saber.

"No need to flash that cheese knife," Fargo said amiably, "we'll do it. But it's going to take a while."

One by one the Henry, the Spencer, the scattergun, and seven handguns counting Fargo's Colt, landed in the grass.

"That bowie knife in your boot, too," the officer told Fargo.

"Lieutenant Woodbine," Sergeant McGreevey said tactfully, "that's called an Arkansas toothpick or a hog-sticker. A bowie has a wider blade."

The lieutenant flushed under his peach fuzz. "Never mind the nomenclature. Corporal Manning! Gather up these weapons and issue these men a receipt for them."

Fargo said, "I take it we're under arrest, Lieutenant?"

"No, sir, you're under official detention by order of the commanding officer."

McGreevey managed to ride close beside Fargo as they rode into the fort.

"Is the C.O. still Lieutenant Colonel Duran?" Fargo asked him.

The sergeant's face looked grim. "Duran's teaching at the academy in West Point now, Skye. Colonel Hiram Pettigrew took over here."

Fargo frowned so deeply his eyebrows touched.

"'S'matter?" Dub asked. "Is that bad?"

"It ain't good," Fargo replied. "You see, his wife's a lot younger than he is—and a lot prettier."

Dub and Nate exchanged glances. Dub said, "And you . . .?"

"A gentleman never tells," Fargo evaded.

"That means he did," Dub said. "And the colonel knows?"

"Rumors," Fargo said cryptically.

They rode through the gate. A large brush ramada shaded the front of the headquarters building. In front of the stables about a dozen horses were feeding at a hayrack.

"That pretty palomino," Fargo said to McGreevey, "let me guess—Belloch's horse, right?"

The sergeant nodded.

"What'd I tell you?" Fargo said to Dub and Nate. "I told you that sissy would ride a lady-broke horse."

"Dismount!" the lieutenant ordered. "McGreevey, Manning, Shoemaker, and Collins—you are guard detail. Keep your weapons on these men at all times in the colonel's office, and if necessary, shoot to kill. Johnson, see to their horses."

"One second, Lieutenant," Fargo said. "With your permission, I'd like to remove a pouch from my near-side saddlebag. It's a military communiqué that the colonel needs to see."

"In that case, I'll remove it. Men, take the prisoners—I mean, detainees inside."

The moment Fargo was "escorted" into the C.O.'s office his gaze fell on a dapper, slender man with a waxed mustache and spade beard. He showed no hardships from the trail, and his suit was neatly brushed and pressed.

"Well," Belloch said when he spotted the ragtag Fargo, "a bad penny always turns up."

Fargo sniffed that lilac hair tonic that Cindy Henning had mentioned. "I'll take a bad penny over a whorehouse."

"Gentlemen," snapped a paunchy, middle-aged soldier with silver muttonchops, seated behind a kneehole desk, "avoid personalities. I am interested only in the truth."

Colonel Pettigrew's coldly autocratic manner had earned him the moniker "Old Sobersides." Fargo slacked into the only empty chair and folded his arms over his chest. The boys remained standing, their features tight with anxiety.

Moss sat along the opposite wall beside his boss, tugging at his eye patch. Like the boys his features were drawn and serious—unlike the cool and collected Belloch.

Pettigrew eyed Fargo with distaste. "Fargo, sometime ago I received a very serious report from Mr. Rafe Belloch here."

"Rafe?" Fargo cut in. "You sure it ain't Rape? That's more like it."

Anger tightened Pettigrew's lips and face. He aimed a quelling stare at Fargo.

"This isn't a barracks-room bull session, Fargo, your very life is on the line. Mr. Belloch has a high position with the Kansas-Pacific Railroad Consortium. He and four witnesses signed a sworn statement that they witnessed you and a band of hooligans attack a group of Quakers west of Sublette. They witnessed numerous murders and rapes. How do you answer this charge?"

"I figured as much," Fargo said calmly. "Now I know how the wind sets. You know, Belloch, you're gonna look right smart when these soldiers fit you with a California collar. You, too, Moss—or should I call you Dead-eye?"

Pettigrew stood up, banging the desk with his fist. "Button your ears back, Fargo, because I'm only going to say it once— *I'm* running these proceedings. Now, how do you answer the charge?"

"All right, then, Colonel, I'll skip the twaddle and bunkum and give it to you straight—Belloch was in charge of that attack on the Quakers, and Moss what's-his-name here was with him. Belloch led a group of about thirty border ruffians from the eastern Kansas Territory, most likely Baxter Springs. Me and these two lads here killed about half of them and put the rest to rout."

"Fargo, that's preposterous," Pettigrew scoffed. "You just heard me tell you Mr. Belloch works for the Kansas-Pacific, and he has credentials to prove it. Why in God's name would he want a massacre along his employer's proposed route?"

"Because this opera-house dandy is sailing under false colors, Colonel. He used to work for the Kansas-Pacific, and no doubt they believe he is. But I'd wager he's secretly working for the Rock Island line, sabotaging the Kansas-Pacific's bid for a transcontinental route."

Pettigrew snorted. "Fargo, you seem to have more conclusions than facts to warrant them."

"What's he got but a pack of lies and no proof? Why, his only 'witness' is that jackal dressed in butternut-dyed homespun—the uniform of the jayhawker marauders."

"Colonel, this is all bluff and bluster," Belloch cut in. "I had three more witnesses until this mad-dog killer started to systematically murder them."

"Nothing ruins truth like stretching it," Fargo said. "All those so-called witnesses are on his payroll. And he's right—I have been trying to kill his men. In fact, I've killed most of his topkicks. That's a natural reaction when killers are throwing lead at me."

"Look at him, Colonel," Belloch said in his suave baritone. "Dried blood on the fringes of his buckskins. And he hasn't even combed his beard in days. He's just some greasy drifter who would kill for two bits. In contrast, I have friends and business associates back in Washington City who have the ear of President Buchanan."

"And who has the ear of Senator Drummond?" Fargo asked casually. "Is it in your pocket, or does Moss have it on that string he took off his belt before riding to the fort?"

"That's a damn lie!" Moss burst out. "It was Jake Ketchum who had that string of—"

"Shut up," Rafe snapped. "He's just goading you."

Throughout this meeting, Rafe Belloch's self-satisfied smirk and air of cool confidence had irked Fargo. Now he had the momentary satisfaction of seeing the murdering scut had turned pale.

"Fargo!" Pettigrew bellowed. "Has your brain come unhinged? I'm having you slapped in irons if you continue these disruptions!"

"You're the ramrod," Fargo said. "But before you do, I think the lieutenant has something you need to see."

# 19

Colonel Pettigrew took a clasp knife from the top drawer of his desk and slit through the sinew thread sealing the pouch.

"There's dried blood on it," he remarked to Fargo.

"The military courier who delivered it," Fargo explained, "was wounded. He died shortly after delivering it."

"To you?"

"No, sir. To a Quaker couple named Emmerick. Mrs. Esther Emmerick asked me to deliver it to a military officer, as the courier requested."

"This is a stunt, Colonel," Belloch protested. "I told you yesterday that Fargo would ride in here with an ace up his sleeve. He has to take the heat off himself for that raid on the Quakers."

Belloch had regained his confident manner, but Fargo noticed how Moss was sweating and fidgeting.

"Looks to me," Fargo remarked, "like Belloch already knows what's in that pouch—Moss, too. That man can't sit still."

"You're out of line, mister," Pettigrew told Fargo.

"I notice how lilac water over there is never out of line—just me. How many hostile Indian camps has he scouted for the U.S. Army?"

Pettigrew ignored this, eyes riveted to the single, handwritten page. It had been scrawled hastily, without benefit of blotting, and he had to pause several times while reading it aloud:

"It's dated September 5, 1860. 'To whomever shall read this report, greetings. I seriously doubt that this missive will ever reach military channels, but I do know it will be my last attempt to contact the outside world. The facts are these: Four days ago I received word, from Rafe Belloch's private dispatch rider, that Belloch needed to confer with Senator Drummond's fact-finding party regarding terrain features affecting the proposed Kansas-

Pacific railroad route. The rider provided map coordinates that took us about forty miles northwest of Sublette.

"'As we approached the rendezvous point, Rafe Belloch emerged from a tent to greet us. Suddenly he screamed "Now!" and, on both sides of us, armed men popped up from cleverly covered rifle pits and commenced a savage enfilade fire.'"

Fargo and the McCallister boys exchanged a quick glance—they, too, had faced one of those clever rifle pits.

"'Senator Drummond was killed instantly and our horses were shot out from under us to prevent our escape. I and five of my surviving men retreated to our two fodder wagons, which we managed to turn on their side and form a crude breastworks. I personally watched Belloch scalp Senator Drummond and mutilate him in the style of Southern Cheyenne Indians. We are nearly out of ammunition, and most of us have been wounded, including myself. Surrender is not an option, after what we witnessed, and we will fight to the death. The sun is setting, and one of my brave lads will try and slip out with this report. Otherwise, the world will never know about the heinous atrocity committed here this day.

"'I commend my soul to my Maker and pray I will die a brave soldier.'"

Colonel Pettigrew looked up and cleared his throat, visibly shaken. "It's signed Brigadier General Daniel Hoffman."

"Barbaric treachery!" exclaimed the lieutenant, starting toward Belloch.

"As you were, Woodbine," the colonel said. "Well, Belloch?"

"Colonel, isn't it obvious what's going on here? Fargo may look rustic, but he's not stupid. Once he realized I witnessed his vicious assault on the Quakers, he knew he had to one-up me. He wrote this letter himself—in fact, it's quite possible that he and his gang of thugs did the very thing he's accusing me of in this so-called 'report.'"

"Preposterous. Fargo's a scoundrel, of sorts, but to be candid, Belloch, I never even believed he attacked the Quakers."

Belloch shook his head. "Oh, it may sound preposterous, but what does anybody really know about Fargo? The man is a notorious loner, and any man who spends too much time alone doesn't think like the majority."

"Belloch, you're cutting it pretty thin," Fargo said. "Colonel, his whole story is moonshine. More full of holes than a strainer. For one thing, just match the signature."

"Colonel, signatures are copied all the time," Belloch pointed out.

"What did I copy it from?" Fargo countered.

"In any event," Pettigrew said, "we have no copies of it on file here at Fort Hays. Before he was assigned to the War Department as an engineering officer, General Hoffman served for years in the Department of New Mexico. We'd have to send for his signature by courier. All five of you men will remain in the guardhouse until this matter can be cleared up. And God have mercy on the guilty ones because I won't."

Just then, outside, Fargo heard iron-rimmed tires scraping the hard-packed dirt of the parade deck.

"Colonel Pettigrew?" he said. "Permission to glance through your window?"

The officer frowned. "Why? There's no possibility of escape, Fargo."

"Just humor me, sir. There's four carbines trained on me."

"If he attempts to leap out that window," Pettigrew ordered the sentries, "kill him. Flight is proof of guilt."

Fargo crossed the office and looked out the open sash window. "Colonel, the matter is about to be wrapped up with a pink ribbon. The Quakers have just arrived from Sublette. Mrs. Emmerick, the woman who gave me that pouch, is driving the wagon that just rolled through the gate."

From the corner of his eye, Fargo saw Belloch's cocky face finally turn into a mask of desperation. Moss looked like a man staring into the pit of hell.

"Mrs. Emmerick!" Fargo called out. "Over here! It's Skye Fargo. Please report to the commanding officer's headquarters right now."

Fargo turned away from the window, grinning like an undertaker after a saloon shootout. "*Now* we'll see where I got that pouch. There's a couple dozen Quakers to back her up."

This was the final straw for Moss. He leaped to his feet. "Colonel, I ain't gonna hang with this slick son of a bitch Belloch. Fargo's telling the straight."

Fargo could almost whiff the rage coming off Belloch.

"Belloch planned the attack on that senator! He—"

All guns had been collected when the civilians rode in, but Belloch's boot dagger was hidden by his pants leg. In a heartbeat he leaped up and tossed it straight into Moss Harper's heart, dropping him to the puncheon floor like a sack of potatoes.

"Don't shoot!" Belloch shouted at the soldiers. "Colonel, I can make you and every man in this room rich beyond his wildest dreams—you, too, Fargo. I'm talking tens of thousands of dollars for all of you."

Pettigrew met Fargo's eyes, and Fargo nodded slightly to signal his understanding.

"Oh?" Pettigrew said. "That sounds promising . . . Rafe. I have no particular fondness for politicians. But how can we be sure you have such funds?"

"Sir, I protest," Lieutenant Woodbine cut in.

"Shut up, shavetail. It can't hurt to hear the man out."

"Of course I don't have the funds with me," Belloch said. "But Fargo hit the nail on the head—secretly I work for the Rock Island Line. They'll pay plenty to put the kibosh on a scandal like this."

Pettigrew nodded. "I see. Well, I've heard all I need to hear. Sergeant McGreevey?"

"Sir?"

"Would you demonstrate the horizontal butt stroke for these two young colts with Fargo?"

"With pleasure, sir."

Before Belloch even realized it was coming, McGreevey smashed the butt plate of his carbine into the railroad agent's mouth. Several pieces of broken teeth rattled onto the floor, and Belloch flew back hard into his chair, screeching in pain.

"Put him in the guardhouse," Pettigrew ordered. "And, Sergeant, if he needs to be . . . disciplined a bit during the night, so be it. Just make sure he's fully aware at his hanging tomorrow morning. Drag that body out, too, and leave it on the plains for carrion bait."

"You can't hang me," Belloch sputtered from a bloody, swelling mouth. "I have a right to be tried in the States."

"You're a better murderer than you are a legal scholar, Belloch. Under territorial law I have the authority of summary punishment once a confession is obtained in front of witnesses. And not only did Harper confess, you just did so de facto. No—you'll get the black gown right here, where no Philadelphia lawyer hired by your employers will get you out on hocus-pocus. Guards, get him out of here before I shoot this piece of scum myself."

"Well, Fargo," the colonel said when Belloch had been dragged away. "Where is Mrs. Emmerick?"

"I'm damned if I know," Fargo confessed. "That was just one of your work details coming in."

Pettigrew's jaw dropped in astonishment. A moment later he, Fargo, and the McCallister boys laughed without restraint for a good ten seconds.

"Fargo," Pettigrew said when he recovered, "my officers have bragged up your ability to bluff at poker. Now I see your reputation is well deserved. I owe you and these boys an apology."

"Apology not accepted, Colonel. Hell, you couldn't know what was going on. Not with a slick weasel like Belloch in the mix. You were doing your job."

"Thanks. I saw a dispatch sometime back. Aren't you supposed to be in the Department of Nebraska by now as an express rider?"

"I was on my way, sir, when my trail crossed Belloch's."

"I see. Do you still want the job?"

"Well, I'm a mite light in the pockets and need paying work."

Pettigrew nodded. "You three looked bushed. Rest here tonight. Get some hot food in you and get cleaned up. I'll authorize rations for the trail, and for you, Fargo, I'll prepare a letter explaining everything. Believe me, the man who ran down General Hoffman's killer will get any job he wants with the army."

"'Preciate that, sir. I really do. And I'd take it kindly if you'd mention Dub and Nate McCallister in that letter, too. I couldn't've done it without these two fellows."

Fargo and the boys started to leave. Pettigrew's voice stopped them. "Fargo . . . Skye?"

Fargo turned around. "Sir?"

"You are obviously an intelligent man—you just proved it with that window trick. Your talents are wasted on this godforsaken frontier. Trade in those buckskins, and I could place you high up in army administration. The world is passing you by. Do you realize we now have a transatlantic cable linking this nation to Europe?"

"I've heard of it, Colonel, but you see, I don't know anybody in Europe. And I'd sooner lose a jaw tooth than give up my buckskins."

Pettigrew smiled. "I think I understand. You're a member of that gallant, hardheaded lot known as the western trailsman."

"That's what some call me," Fargo agreed, tossing the colonel a salute before he left.

# 20

Upon learning that Nate's black had been shot out from under him by Moss Harper, Colonel Pettigrew presented him with Rafe Belloch's palomino. Despite Fargo's suspicion of "pretty" horses, he had to agree the gelding was a strong, well-trained mount of good disposition.

"Just a word of advice, though," Fargo told Nate as the trio rode out from Fort Hays. "Pry those silver conchos off the saddle. They're fancy, all right, but they reflect light for miles. And Indians love to track down reflections."

"Mr. Fargo," Dub said. "What'd you think of the hanging this morning?"

"Usually I'm one to avoid them. I take no pleasure in watching a man die. But with Rafe Belloch it was different. That's one necktie sociable I truly enjoyed."

"Do they usually puke and beg for mercy like that?"

"His kind generally do, except they usually piss themselves during the hanging."

Four days of steady, uneventful riding brought them to Sublette, where they picked up the two dobbins under Enis Hagan's care at the trading post.

"Let me take a wild guess," Hagan greeted them. "Rafe Belloch and his lick-spittles are worm fodder now?"

"You can chisel that in granite," Fargo assured him. "But there'll be more like him sure as flies buzzing around your molasses barrel."

"That's what Rosario decided. She hired a guide and she's on her way back to Mexico City."

They covered the thirty miles to the McCallister place under a pearl gray sky. But a mile from the failed farm, a huge raft of clouds blew away from the sun, bathing the Great Plains in a luminous, golden aura.

"You was right, Mr. Fargo," Dub said, gazing over the almost infinite vista. "There is somethin' sorta . . . majestic about the open spaces."

Fargo nodded. "It doesn't take your breath away like the Sierras or the Yellowstone country. But eventually it sneaks up on a man."

The faithful old hound, Dan'l Boone, announced their arrival before they entered the barren windswept yard.

"Well, Skye," Lorena greeted him. "I see you brought my wayward boys home."

"Your wayward men," Fargo corrected her as he lit down and loosened the Ovaro's girth. "I'd be proud to ride the river with them any day. In fact, I owe them my life. They got the job done, Lorena, and never showed their back to the enemy."

The boys were fairly bursting with pride at such praise. Lorena hugged each of them, her eyes filming with tears of joy at their safe return.

"Say . . . where's Cindy?" Dub asked, adding hastily: "And Krissy?"

"They walked the five miles to the Westphal place. Boys, I've been thinking—Skye is right. We're too far west too early. The Westphals are giving up and heading back to the States. They've invited me, Krissy, and Cindy to go with them. I sent the girls over to tell them we will. It's just not safe for women out here. I can't tell you boys—you young men—what to do. But I pray God the family will stay together."

Dub and Nate exchanged a long, uncertain glance.

"Do you mean to tell me," Fargo said to them sternly, "that two experienced plainsmen like you are going to let your mother and two young ladies cross the Great American Desert without your protection? The two of you alone are worth a squad of cavalry."

"'Course we ain't," Dub said. "Look what happened to Cindy."

"Then it's settled," Lorena said, beaming. "Now ride over to the Westphal place and bring Krissy and Cindy home. Neither of those girls has decent shoes."

"Good-bye, Mr. Fargo!" Nate called as the brothers rode out. "Good luck up north!"

"Stay frosty!" Dub added, and Fargo grinned.

"So you're on your way, Skye?" Lorena said.

"Reckon so. I owe the army some work."

"Well, at least come in for a glass of applejack before you go."

"I wouldn't mind cutting the dust," Fargo agreed, following the shapely widow into the barn. One corner served as a kitchen, with an oilcloth-covered table, a hand pump, and crossed-stick shelves. Fargo took a seat on a keg while she poured the applejack from a crockery jug, her unrestrained russet hair brushing his hand.

"You know," she said with a mischievous smile, "after you and Krissy went out to the bathing pool? That girl walked around in a daze for almost a week."

Fargo choked on his applejack.

"Oh, I'm not angry," she hastened to add. "Just envious of these young girls. I know this is bold and forward talk, Skye, but you're leaving and—and it's been five years since I've felt a man against my bare skin. I've missed that feeling. But surely men like you don't look twice at worn-out dish rags like me. Why would you?"

"I've looked more than twice at you, Lorena. And I don't see any dishrag. Just fine linen cloth."

"You mean . . . you'd be willing?"

"Willing, able—" He stood up. "And as you can see, ready."

She stared at the impressive tent in his trousers. "My, are you ready! No wonder Krissy daydreams for hours."

Fargo took her hand and led her toward the beds. "Nothing against these lovely twenty-year-olds," he told her. "But there's nothing quite like a *woman*."

**LOOKING FORWARD!**
**The following is the opening
section of the next novel in the exciting
*Trailsman* series from Signet:**

**THE TRAILSMAN #345
SOUTH PASS SNAKE PIT**

*South Pass, Wind River Range, 1859—where a valley of death
is littered with the skeletons of children,
and Fargo discovers the only god around is Sam Colt.*

"More trouble already," Skye Fargo muttered to his horse, "and
we haven't even got there yet. Bad omen."

The lean, tall, hard-knit man clad in fringed buckskins sat his
stallion at the summit of South Pass, brass field glasses trained
on a crude camp in the center of narrow Sweetwater Valley below
him. Hills surrounded the valley on all sides with magnificent
white mountain peaks like spires ranging in a curtain-fold pat-
tern behind them.

For the moment, however, Fargo ignored the natural beauty
of western Wyoming, the Indian name he preferred for this re-
mote corner of the vast Nebraska Territory. Instead, his lips a grim,
determined slit visible in a close-cropped brown beard, he watched
the sadistic scene unfolding below at the edge of the camp.

Four or five bully-boy types—wearing their guns below their
hips in the style of stone-cold killers—were tying an elderly man

to a tree. The victim was scrawny and his unhealthy skin looked like yellowed ivory.

Fargo gave a long, fluming sigh. "There goes our big plan for riding in unnoticed," he told his black-and-white pinto. "Good chance they plan to kill that old boy if we don't stop it. Gee up!"

Fargo cursed the luck. He had been paid generously to solve a mystery for a man who was literally dying of grief—a man he respected greatly. He had hoped to join the community below and blend in. That seemed unlikely now.

He headed for a crude trail, just ahead, that led down into the valley. He was at the southern end of the Wind River Range where it opened on to South Pass, the crucial gateway discovered by Jim Bridger that opened up the Far West to the Oregon Trail.

Here at the summit, the pass was an almost level saddle about four miles wide from north to south. Beyond the pass, to the north, tiers of rock ledges, stretches of pine, and pockets of gray sage led to the foothills and the snow-peaked mountains beyond. To the south, Fargo spotted large boulders where migrating pilgrims had chiseled their names. But it was well into September now, too late to clear the mountains before the snowfall, and there was no sign of the canvas-covered bone-shakers making the transmontane journey.

"Step easy, old campaigner," Fargo advised his Ovaro as he tugged rein and they started down the only trail into the valley. He knew from experience it was just a sandy and rocky trace with washouts that had to be detoured. At one point it turned into an unstable landslide slope, but the Ovaro, sure-footed as a mule, got them across safely.

Soon Fargo didn't need his spy glasses to see what was going on. The camp, while sprawling, was still far from being a town. Tents, log huts, and several flimsy structures of rough-milled lumber were scattered along a wide, wagon-rutted street. Good building material was scarce thanks to a lack of sawmills, and roofing was as simple as old vegetable cans flattened into shingles.

However, one new house of obviously imported milled lumber stood above the camp on a grassy bench.

*There's where the king coyote lives,* Fargo told himself. *There's one heap big chief in every roach pit.*

"I said talk out, goddamn it!" shouted a thickset bull of a man with a face hard as granite. "Talk out or I'll peel your back like an onion."

The granite-faced man snapped a long blacksnake whip, opening a bloody crease in the prisoner's back. He loosed a yawp of pain.

"I don't know what you're talking about!" the elderly man protested.

"Like hob you don't, you milk-kneed school man. Tell us about the box."

Fargo gigged the Ovaro forward. The granite-faced man with the whip wore a bright red sash around his waist. Two ivory-handled .36 caliber Colt 1851 Navy revolvers were tucked in, butts forward. One of the four men watching also wore two guns in cutaway holsters, a pair of .38 Colt revolvers. A man out west, Fargo knew, could wear one gun or none. But two were the mark of either a grandstander or a killer.

"Hold on," Fargo called out as red sash raised the whip.

Hard-bitten eyes watched Fargo as he hauled back on the reins.

"Well, look-a-here, boys," red sash said, his tone mocking. "A true-blue, blown-in-the-bottle frontiersman! Jasper shits in the woods, hanh? They call you Boone or Crockett, stranger?"

"Wearin' buckskins with bloody fringes," said a man with a string-bean build. "Must be Joe Shit the Ragman, can't even afford white man's duds. Betcha he's gone to the blanket, got hisself a squaw."

Fargo ignored the others, watching the apparent leader of this pack of curs. "This man's too old to go under the lash."

"Brash as a government mule, ain't he?" the man with the whip said to this companions. "Stranger, it's no say-so of yours what we do with this white-livered pus bag. You one of them mushy-headed do-gooders?"

"No. But once, at Cherry Creek mining camp, an old gent who looks just like him cut a Cheyenne arrow point out of my back."

String bean: "Well, this old soak ain't him, squaw man."

"It's true that I imbibe infrequent potations from a bottle," protested the scrawny prisoner, "but I'm certainly no drunk."

"Shut your piehole," red sash snapped. "You don't just drink—you're a pipe through the floor."

He looked at Fargo. "Who asked you to shoot off your chin, stranger?"

"I'm just trying to help the old gent out, that's all."

"Yeah? Well who are you, and what the hell you doing here? Men don't just end up in Sweetwater Valley by happenchance."

"I got a brother missing," Fargo lied. "He's a trapper like me. We were s'posed to meet at Sitwell's Creek east of here, but he never showed. He was running traps along the Sweetwater River, so I decided to give the area a squint."

"Trapper, huh? Beaver's been trapped out for twenty years."

Fargo nodded. "We go for red and silver fox. The pelts sell high back in Saint Louis."

The leader moved a few paces to get a better look under the wide brim of Fargo's black plainsman's hat. "Say . . . your map is familiar. You ever been to Silver City in New Mexico Territory?"

The question jogged Fargo's memory too—the speaker was the notorious Jack Slade. But Fargo continued to lie with a poker face. He shook his head. "Did some trapping near Taos, is all."

String bean pointed at Fargo's Arkansas toothpick. "That pig sticker in your boot ain't worth a Chinese whisker around here. You're among gun hands now, squaw man."

Fargo turned his head and looked at the man from calm, fathomless eyes. "I've been keeping accounts on you, old son. Your tongue swings way too loose."

"I didn't catch you name," Slade pressed.

"John Doe."

"You're hanging by a thread, stranger. Before you start rocking the boat, you better take the temperature of the water. Clay!"

"Yo!"

A surly-mouthed young man whose jet-black hair was slicked back with axle grease stepped closer. He was the one, Fargo noticed, wearing the pair of .38 Colt revolvers.

"John Doe, meet Clay Munro," Slade said. "He was raised from birth to eat six-shooters. Clay, give Mr. Doe here a little preview of what's in store for him if he don't light a shuck outta this valley."

Two bullet-riddled oyster cans sat in the rutted street about seventy yards away. Munro slapped leather with both hands and opened fire, one gun trained on each can as he emptied the wheels. Both cans rolled and bounced, not one bullet missing its target.

"Can you tie that, John Doe?" Slade demanded.

"What's the difference?" Fargo replied. "Oyster cans don't shoot back."

"You're a hard customer, eh?"

"I don't talk about what I am. I just do what I have to."

By now several of the thugs were shuffling their feet in a way Fargo recognized—they were nerving up to kill him. All his plans to slip into the valley quietly were smoke behind him. Now he had to take the bull by the horns, and quick.

"His tough horseshit talk don't fool me none," String bean said, his mouth curling into a sneer. "Squaw boy here is just whistling past the graveyard. I'm gonna bore him through right now. And I get first dibs on that Henry rifle in his saddle boot."

"Dibs on the stallion," Clay Munro said.

Fargo's lake blue eyes watched String bean, unblinking. "Let's clarify this point. Are you threatening to kill me?"

"Goddamn straight I am, buckskin boy. You're about to buck out."

"Jesse," the red-sashed leader cut in, "ease off. I got a hunch I know who this gazabo is."

"Don't matter to me if he's the Queen of England. I'm sending this bastard across the mountains."

"Well, we can't have that now, can we?" Fargo said almost cheerfully.

Quicker than thought, Fargo filled his hand with blue steel and felt the Colt jump. His bullet opened a neat hole in Jesse's forehead, and the corpse flopped hard to the ground like a sack of mail.

"Well, for sweet Jesus!" exclaimed the prisoner tied to the tree.

"Clay!" the leader shouted when the young target shooter's hands started for his guns. "I know who this jasper is. His name's Skye Fargo—better known as the Trailsman."

All four men stared in slack-jawed idiocy at the lifeless heap, blood still pooling in the dirt.

Fargo had already thumb-cocked the single-action Colt. Wisps of powder smoke still curled from the muzzle. "Anybody else want the balance of these pills? If you do, clear leather."

Evidently no one did.

"I ain't never heard of no Fargo," Clay said. "And anyhow, that was cold-blooded murder!"

"You best study up on territorial law, junior," Fargo advised. "It's called 'no duty to retreat.' Any man receiving a direct threat to his life is in immediate danger and can kill in self-defense."

The kid looked at Slade. "Is that the straight?"

Slade nodded. "'Fraid so."

"Hell, mister, men make threats like that all the time."

Fargo's lips eased back off his teeth. "Not to me they don't."

"I pegged you all wrong, Fargo," Slade admitted. "You're a hard twist, all right."

"Only when I'm forced to it."

"You're a nervy cuss," Clay conceded. "But, mister, we own this valley. You'd be wise to show this camp your dust."

"I just did when I rode in," Fargo said. "You'll see it again when I choose to leave. Ain't no man allowed to own one inch of territorial land—not until the government passes this Homestead Act. Now, all you boys just clear out of my gun sights, and drag your dead pard with you."

"The worm will turn, Fargo," Clay Munro vowed. "I'm going to—"

"Clay!" Jack Slade cut him off, pointing at the dead man. "There's no education in the second kick of a mule."

Clay took the point and avoided any threats.

"Fargo," Slade said, "I don't believe for one minute you're here to find a brother. And you sure don't set up like no trapper. A man as gun handy and cool nerved as you could be mighty useful to the rainmaker in this valley, an hombre named Philly Denton. Let me know and I'll set up a meeting."

"I'll keep that in mind," Fargo said, still holding his Colt.